Wishing STONE

THE STONE SERIES: BOOK FOUR

USA TODAY BESTSELLING AUTHOR

DAKOTA WILLINK

PRAISE FOR THE STONE SERIES

"There's a new billionaire in town! Fans of Fifty Shades and Crossfire will devour this series!"
— **After Fifty Shades Book Blog**

"It's complex. It's dirty. And I relished every single detail. This series is going to my TBR again and again!"
— **Not Your Moms Romance Blog**

"This read demanded to be heard. It screamed escape from the everyday and gave me that something extra I was looking for."
— **The Book Junkie Reads**

"Hang on to your kindles! It's a wild ride!"
— **Once Upon An Alpha**

"A definite page turner with enticing romance scenes that will make you sweat even during those cold winter nights!"
— **Redz World**

Library of Congress Cataloging-in-Publication Data

ISBN-13: 978-1-954817-18-0

Wishing Stone | Copyright © 2021 by Dakota Willink | Pending

Cover Design by: Dragonfly Ink Publishing Copyright © 2021

Editing by: Cheryl Maddox, Dragonfly Ink Publishing

Formatting by: Dragonfly Ink Publishing

WISHING STONE

THE STONE SERIES: BOOK 4

DAKOTA WILLINK

AUTHOR NOTE

Dear Readers,

It's been four years since the release of *Set In Stone*, book 3 in *The Stone Series*. Since then, I've had many fans send emails asking if I would ever add to Krystina and Alexander's story. So, this past summer, I revisited the idea and plotted the next part of their journey.

I asked myself, where are they now? How much has the world changed for them? Did I want to pick up their story where it left off, or should I fast forward to four years later?

The answer to these questions was not very hard. Alexander and Krystina had never been far from my mind, and I always knew I wasn't quite finished with them. It's also why I called these books a series and not a trilogy.

Ultimately, I decided to bring them into the current world as we know it, making their struggles the same as so many others. After all, New York City has prominence in their world. I'm from New York, and I felt I would be remiss not to mirror Krystina and Alexander's experiences to that of so many New Yorkers.

Once I figured out all the whats, whens, wheres, and whys, I realized this next segment of their story would be a bit longer than initially expected. Because of that, you can consider this a really long prequel that sets the stage for the bigger story that's yet come.

But don't worry—I won't leave you hanging until book five releases. You can count on a happily ever after in *Wishing Stone*!

I hope you enjoy!

— *DAKOTA WILLINK*

"What is Christmas? It is tenderness for the past, courage for the present, hope for the future."

— *AGNES M. PAHRO*

PROLOGUE

Alexander

"Alex, I'm ready. I want to try again," Krystina announced.

My eyes widened in surprise, and my gut instantly clenched. I pivoted in my position at the foot of our custom-made king-sized bed to look at her. My beautiful wife lay naked over the satin sheets on the mattress. Her cheeks were flushed, her mane of chocolate curls tousled from sex, but I didn't afford myself a moment to appreciate her freshly fucked look. I was too busy trying to absorb the shock I felt from her words.

"You can't be serious," I replied, not bothering to keep the incredulity from my voice.

"I've given this a lot of thought. It's been a year. Emotionally, I've had time to heal. I'll never forget what happened, but I don't feel so raw that I can't put it behind me. I want this—I want a family. We deserve it."

Turning away from her, I looked out the balcony doors of our bedroom. The November weather had started out mild but was going out with a vengeance. After three days of downpours and flash flood warnings, the precipitation had changed to freezing rain. The icy droplets beat angrily against the glass, matching my foul mood. Still, nothing could match the torrent of emotions I'd felt a year ago.

I shook my head to clear it, not wanting to remember what it felt like to see Krystina's heart-wrenching tears, knowing I was partly to blame for them. Nevertheless, the effort to block out the painful memories was in vain, and they came flooding in. The calamity was just as devastating as it was when I'd initially experienced it.

The first year after Krystina and I were married, we'd conceived a child twice, but she miscarried both times. It seemed as though I could give her anything her heart longed for—except a viable pregnancy. Then, a year ago, we conceived a child for the third time. However, just like the first two pregnancies, she didn't carry past the first trimester. She had been so sure about the third pregnancy, which only made the loss that much harder.

"What's wrong with me?" she had asked. My heart constricted, unable to forget the crack in her voice when she posed the question. It was as if losing our baby had somehow been her fault—like she was flawed when the reality was that the loss had been because of me. Krystina, my perfect angel, was never to blame for any of it.

I should have been more careful with her.

A few months later, she said she wanted to try again, but I had to consider how the risks had changed. A global pandemic had hit the world, and I couldn't ignore it. The fear of bringing a child into the chaos surrounding us had been all-consuming, and the timing just didn't feel right. In the end, I convinced Krystina to wait before we gave it another go. I'd felt good about the choice, as it had given me a tiny shred of control during a time when everything seemed to be spiraling.

But now, she didn't want to wait anymore.

"Krystina, it's not about whether you've put things behind you or not. You know why we can't. It's not safe."

"Alex, please," she said quietly. My heart constricted when I heard the pain in her voice. "I don't think you understand how I feel. Everything was so chaotic when the pandemic first hit, and I didn't really have time to think about much. My only focus was working out the logistics to transition Turning Stone Advertising to a remote workforce. Once things settled and we established a routine via video conference, I learned that Sara Fink, one of our graphic designers, was pregnant. It was a bittersweet feeling at first, but now seeing her swollen belly through the computer screen just makes me sad. I have this torturous ache in the pit of my stomach whenever I see her. Even seeing a newborn baby on the television gets me all twisted up. I don't want to feel this ache anymore, Alex."

I pressed my lips together in a tight line. The ache she spoke of was something I understood. It came from not having what you longed for more than anything. I wanted this baby just as much as she did. The mere idea of us creating life together left me feeling awestruck. But after everything I had seen, I wasn't ready to risk her safety or the welfare of the child we might conceive without taking additional precautions. I was afraid, and I had every right to be. Krystina didn't understand because had been sheltered from the worst of it, working from home and far away from the city's dense population. She may have seen variations of what was happening on the news, but it was nothing like seeing it firsthand. If she had, she may have shared my concerns.

"Angel, it's you who doesn't understand," I stated pragmatically. "You didn't witness the things I saw and heard—the sounds of sirens on empty streets, the frantic calls from government officials looking to lease warehouse space from Stone Enterprise so they could store personal protective equipment. PPE, they'd called it. I'd learned all the acronyms before you or anyone in the public had even heard of such a thing."

She shook her head, and her frown deepened.

"It's our turn at happiness, Alex. Like I said—we

deserve this. And to be perfectly honest, I think the virus has done its worst. Modern medicine has shown us the light at the end of the tunnel. I truly believe it's safe to try again."

I disagreed, but I knew how Krystina could be when her mind was made up. Turning away from her, I began to pace. My gut clenched from an inexplicable fear as I tried to tamp down the many nightmarish scenarios of something terrible happening to her.

Since the moment I met Krystina, she'd been fiercely independent. I tried to tame her but had failed miserably. She was determined to get what she wanted through her own efforts and means, and she'd never once asked me for anything in the process.

Until now.

I turned back to look at her. She had moved so she was sitting, her back propped up with pillows as she held a sheet over her naked breasts. There was pain in her eyes, but there was no mistaking the determined set to her jaw as well. And at that moment, I knew she'd figure out a way to get what she wanted this time too. If that happened, everything would be out of my control.

That will never do.

If I was going to consider giving in to her desires, I needed to do it on my terms.

"If I agree to this, we'll need to establish some ground rules," I began.

"Okay. Whatever you want," she said, just a little too quickly.

"Don't be so quick to agree, Krystina. Listen to what I have to say first," I warned. "While we are trying to get pregnant and, assuming our efforts are successful, you will need to limit all public exposure for the duration of your pregnancy. You've already been working remotely, but you've been known to pop into the office from time to time for random things. That needs to stop. You cannot go there at all. Workdays will be exclusively remote from this point on."

"That won't be too hard to do."

"Limiting all public exposure also means no more dining out or trips to the store. Nobody is allowed inside the house other than the live-in staff and me—no friends, no family, and certainly no strangers. The staff will also be given safety protocols."

"That's a bit extreme, don't you think?"

I gave her a pointed look.

"Nothing is too extreme when it comes to your safety," I said bluntly.

"So, what you want is for me to be locked up in a gilded cage," she summarized, motioning to the grand house surrounding us with a sweep of her arm. There was a slight curve to her lips, and it was hard to tell if she took my rules seriously or found them amusing. My wife could be hard to read at times—an enigma of sorts—and I couldn't remember a time when I wanted to see into her mind more than I did at that moment.

"Angel, I don't *want* to keep you confined in such a strict way. I need to. You know that, right?"

"I know," she said with resignation. "We've experienced so much loss. I know this is just your way of doing everything you can to minimize the risks of me miscarrying again—or worse."

Moving over to the bed, I sat down next to her and pressed my forehead to hers.

"Sometimes I feel like the world has gone mad, and this is the only way I know how to keep some small measure of control amidst the chaos. You're my angel. I would never survive if something were to happen to you. The only way I will agree to try having a baby again is if you agree to my terms."

She angled her head back, revealing sparkling tears in her eyes. Her lower lip trembled, and I quieted her tumbling breath with a press of my lips. When I pulled away, she smiled.

"I'll do anything if it means we get to begin our family. I love you, Alex." Clasping my face between her palms, she brought her lips to mine once more, effectively sealing our deal.

I should have felt good about the arrangement. After all, I was in control. It was what I'd wanted. But all I felt was trepidation.

1

One Year Later

Alexander

New York was known as the city that never sleeps. That was true—until recently, that is. The blare of taxicab horns seemed a lot less frequent now. It used to take over an hour to get from Soho to Midtown during rush hour, but now one could sometimes make the drive in less than twenty minutes. A lot had changed in just a few short years. I thought I was prepared for it, but some things were impossible to predict.

I mused over all that was different as I pulled from the Cornerstone Tower parking ramp and steered my Tesla

Model S through the streets of Lower Manhattan. The light at the upcoming intersection turned red and I slowed to a stop. Glancing out the window, I took in the festive garland strung between the streetlamps. It connected to each light post with silver bells and holly. I eyed up the storefronts lining the street. A few blocks ahead, there used to be a shop called Indio Banks, a renowned men's fashion designer. The owner had custom-tailored the suit I was currently wearing. Now the shop had empty, dusty windows, matching so many other stores and restaurants in the once bustling city.

The abandoned storefronts were a stark contrast to the curbside Christmas cheer. New York was suffering, and I wondered if she would ever return to being the pulsating and energetic Big Apple that I once knew.

As I drove along the Hudson River, past the Javits Center, and through Hell's Kitchen, I thought about my wife and how sad it would make her when she eventually saw what had become of New York. While there were no more secrets between Krystina and me, I didn't have the heart to tell her how the city she loved so much had changed.

After three and a half years of marriage, we were in a good place, and I would do anything to keep us there. We'd overcome a lot, and there were times when I thought we were strong enough to handle anything. It was all about embracing change, something I usually welcomed. After all, progress wasn't possible without it.

Navigating life's ups and downs was a challenge that I happily took on, recognizing that controlling the direction of the current was the key to achieving my desired results.

Although it hadn't been easy, Krystina had adjusted remarkably well to being married to someone like me. She quickly adapted to the need for privacy and understood how easily we could become a tabloid fixture. The press had always taken an interest in me before, but the paparazzi had become wholly obsessed after I married Krystina. They stalked our every move, and I'd hated that she'd had to suffer through the worst of it. Everything from the clothes she wore to how she styled her hair had been scrutinized in the tabloids. It was maddening. There had been several occasions when I'd come close to slugging a few shady reporters lurking about, but I'd held back thanks to Hale Fulton, the head of my security team.

Hale. Add that to the list of things that had changed.

Hale and I had gone through a rough patch a few years ago, but time proved to heal most wounds. He may have been my security detail for years, but he was so much more than that. I loved him like a father. I just didn't realize how much until I suddenly didn't have the man who'd always been there for me since I was a little boy.

I knew the weight of his betrayal still hung heavy on his shoulders, but ultimately, none of it was his fault. Yes, he had lied to me, but I couldn't hold it against him. He'd been acting out of loyalty, and I would have done exactly as he had if I were in his position.

Still, Hale had noticeably aged after the web of dark lies surrounding my family fell apart. While still physically fit, the retired Navy Commander had begun looking tired, so I'd decided to take him off my personal detail. Instead of being my chauffeur and bodyguard, I had him oversee all security operations, including the property in Westchester, where I'd built a home with Krystina.

After the death of his mother, I suggested Hale move into the guesthouse on the east side of the property. After all his years of service, he deserved the quaint but spacious 2-bedroom home. Plus, I wanted him close to the house while I worked in the city. Paparazzi could often be found near property lines, and after a picture of my half-naked wife lounging by our inground pool had been plastered all over the local tabloids, I wanted to make sure nothing like that happened ever again.

Continuing the hour-long commute home from work, I jumped onto I-87 toward Westchester County until I reached the long winding road that led to home. Freshly fallen snow covered the ground and tree-lined street. It shimmered on the branches from the low-hanging sun. Pulling my sunglasses from the visor, I shielded my eyes from the bright rays bouncing off the tiny white crystals.

I slowed as I approached the concealed private driveway. Then, turning left, I continued up a small hill to where our custom-built home had been constructed three years ago. After much debate over the blueprints, I'd given into Krystina's desires to build a Georgian Colonial made with handpicked stone. I'd wanted her happy above all else, and giving up my contemporary design ideas of steel, concrete, and glass was a small sacrifice to make. Instead, the house had a traditional feel, but I ensured it included all the modern amenities from the original architectural plans I'd commissioned.

Tall pines dusted with white snow flanked both sides of the ten-thousand square feet Chappaqua mansion, making it look like it belonged in a Currier and Ives painting. Smoke billowed from the chimney on the east side of the house, signaling that Vivian, our live-in housekeeper, had lit a fire in one of the four woodburning fireplaces.

I maneuvered the Tesla around the semi-circular driveaway toward the back of the house. Usually, I would have just parked out front and let Hale or Samuel Faye, another security staff member, bring the car to the garage. However, I knew they were currently out surveying the property for any damage that may have occurred to our security systems during a windstorm we'd had a couple of days ago. Because of that, I was on my own today.

When I reached the row of garage doors, I slowed the car to stop, then climbed out and walked up to the lockbox mounted on the exterior wall. After inserting my key, I opened the metal door. A pin pad and a palm scanner were inside the box for extra security. One could never be too careful when owning a Ferrari Sergio and a slew of other luxury vehicles valued high enough to feed a small country. Placing my palm on the glass screen, I waited for it to flash green, then typed in my passcode.

Once the Tesla was parked safely inside the garage, I opted to walk back around to the front of the house rather than go in through the back entrance. There was just something refreshing about the icy air—cleansing almost —and I wanted to breathe it in for a moment longer.

My shoes crunched on the thin layer of snow as I made my way to the front door. When I stepped inside, I was greeted by the sweeping grand staircase, rotunda, and giant windows. Some may view the house as ostentatious. The sheer size of the seven-bedroom colonial could have easily made that accurate, but it never felt empty or without life because of the little touches Krystina sprinkled throughout the rooms. We didn't need to have the plush holiday garland of pine and holly winding up the banister of the grand staircase to bring Christmas cheer. Krystina alone made our house a home—a real home—and someplace I could truly let my guard down.

I inhaled deep and took in the scent of warm apples and cinnamon.

Vivian must be baking.

My life was so very domestic now, and I'd been surprised by how easily I'd adapted to it. But even more shocking was how much I liked it. This house symbolized the evolution of a man. I was no longer the little boy living in a run-down seedy apartment, nor was I the displaced teenager who'd grown up to live a solitary life while amassing a multi-billion-dollar empire. I'd left behind bachelorhood, sex clubs, and the sterile penthouse in Manhattan to embrace the feeling of home for the first time in my life. Without Krystina, that never would have happened. She was my center in all things.

After hanging my coat in the closet, I glanced at my watch. It was just after three in the afternoon. Most likely, Krystina would still be working. I'd left my office at Stone Enterprise in Manhattan early, hoping to surprise her. Crossing the grand foyer, I headed to her office on the second floor. It wasn't a formal office per se but the second floor of the two-story library that she had converted into her workspace, also referred to recently as her command center, for Turning Stone Advertising. She reasoned that there would be plenty of room to spread out ad design plans and mockups for as long as she worked from home.

With each passing month, Krystina spread out further and further until cardboard designs and A-framed easels took up almost the entire library. I abhorred the mess it created. I needed everything neat and orderly while I worked, but Krystina was more like a hurricane in motion whenever she was in the thick of a project, and she often left a trail of destruction in her wake.

The only reason I didn't argue with her about the clutter was because I knew she wasn't thrilled about working from home. Working remotely was only supposed to be a temporary arrangement, but one month had turned into two, and two had turned into twelve. Then I'd put my restrictions in place while we tried to get pregnant. Without a proper workspace, her mess was inevitable. I just made sure to avoid that area of the house as much as possible.

When I reached the top of the staircase, I made my way down the hall toward the library's second floor. Sliding open the pocket mahogany doors to the library, I found the space empty. She wasn't at her desk, nor was she standing near the line of posterboard easels that lined the far wall.

"Krystina? Angel, I'm home," I called out.

When there was no answer, the stomach-churning fear I felt was instant. Krystina had been alone far too much this past year and I knew it was starting to take a toll on her. Several times over the past few weeks, I'd caught her crying for unknown reasons. I was beginning to grow more and more concerned—especially after the way I'd found her last week. I shuddered from the memory of her weeping in the room that would one day be a nursery for our future children. She'd been upset over what could be and what had unfairly been taken away.

Now, here we were, a year into her confinement, and my wife still wasn't pregnant. I wasn't sure how much longer this could go on. I knew being completely homebound made her days feel long, and I was beginning to worry about the isolation. I feared depression might be impacting her ability to conceive. If I had one wish this Christmas, it would be to give her the baby she so desperately wanted.

Moving quickly down the hall, I headed toward the bedrooms. Opening the door to the future nursery, I hoped I wouldn't find her there in tears once again. When I saw that she wasn't there either, I audibly sighed with relief but wondered where she could be.

I pursed my lips in annoyance, suddenly missing the open floorplan of my Manhattan penthouse for the first time in years. While Krystina and I had decided to keep the penthouse, we only stayed there on occasion when in the city later than usual. At least there, a person would be easy to find. Whereas here, with all its rooms and passageways, a person could easily hide for a week.

I went back downstairs and checked the den and family room, two of the places Krystina would often curl up and read the latest crime and mystery novel. She wasn't there, nor was she in the breakfast nook where we took most of our meals. Moving into the main kitchen area, I spotted Vivian at the large center island where she had formed several small piles of white flour into mini volcano-shaped craters. I had no idea what she was making, but I was sure that whatever it was would be phenomenal.

"Hello, Mr. Stone. You're home early," she observed as

she cracked an egg and dropped the yolks into one of the flour depressions. "I hope you're hungry. I'm making homemade ravioli for dinner tonight, and I've got apple crisp baking for dessert."

"That sounds great, Vivian," I replied absently. "Have you seen Krystina?"

"Yes, sir. She's in the living room. From the state of things, I think she's feeling pretty festive too."

"Oh? Why do you say that?"

"She received a rather large delivery today, and she's been grinning ear to ear ever since. It's nice to see her smiling. Go see for yourself."

Feeling perplexed, I did as Vivian suggested and went to the formal living room. When I reached it, I felt Krystina before I saw her. It was the connection we had—the one that could make my synapses fire in a million directions. Only my wife had the ability to light up all the places inside me that had been dark for most of my life.

Today, she was standing on the bottom rung of a ladder, surrounded by boxes, ribbons, and ornaments. Everything was strewn about as she attempted to put together a pre-lit artificial tree that was three times her height. Her long curly brown hair was pulled back into a loose ponytail, leaving just a few waves free to frame her beautiful face. She wore a baggy off-the-shoulder white sweater over tight jeans, and her hips swayed to the tune of Dean Martin's *Baby, It's Cold Outside*. She looked like an angel—albeit an angel surrounded by absolute chaos—

but she was my angel, nonetheless. I couldn't help but chuckle at the sight.

She glanced my way when she heard me laugh, and her face lit up as she stepped off the ladder. She seemed to glow in the sparkling twinkle lights of the tree, emphasizing her beauty in a way that took my breath away.

Crossing the room, I pulled her to my chest and kissed the top of her head, clinging to her for a moment longer than I usually would have. My need for her had always been just as strong as the first day we met, but today seemed amplified—as if I couldn't be close enough to her.

"You're home early," she murmured.

"I missed you, angel." Leaning in, I pressed my lips to hers.

Her body easily gave in, her hands reaching up to clasp the back of my neck. I growled my appreciation of her welcoming kiss as my lips melded with hers. I kissed her deeply, our tongues sliding, clashing, then savoring. This was home—the taste of her lips, the feel of her fingers in my hair. Everything about her was real and urgent every single time we were together.

Almost reluctantly, I pulled away. Reaching up, I traced the line of her bottom lip with my finger. "If I'd known I would get a welcome like that, I'd have been home sooner."

She smiled and swatted playfully at my arm. "I kiss you like that almost every time you come home."

"I know. I'm a lucky man," I said with a devilish wink, then motioned to the mess all over the living room. "So, tell me. What's all of this?"

"I'm decorating."

"I can see that, but...." I trailed off and frowned, suddenly realizing what was different about the Christmas tree. "That's a fake tree. Why didn't you get a real one?"

"Because I couldn't leave the house to pick one out."

A sharp stab of guilt poked at my chest, knowing that was her subtle way of reminding me about the rules I'd dictated to keep her safe.

"We had one delivered last year, remember?" I reminded. "We just took a walk around the property while the crew was inside setting it up so there was no risk of exposing you to anything."

"Oh, I remember it vividly. After they left, Vivian ran around the house spraying disinfectant. I ended up tasting it for a week," she said with a wry smile. "But to be perfectly honest, I wasn't happy with last year's tree. It was short and lopsided even though we'd asked for a tall one to reach these soaring ceilings. That tree was anything but."

I pursed my lips together and frowned as I recalled seeing last year's tree for the first time. Krystina was right. It had been very crooked and not nearly as tall as it was supposed to be. Had I been in the house when it arrived, I would have sent it back. While she tried to hide the worst of the cockeyed angle by positioning the tree in a corner, it was still bad.

Nevertheless, Krystina loved Christmas, and there were specific must-do's every year. Having a real tree was one of them.

"Angel, you've always insisted on having a real tree. Are you sure this is what you want?"

"It's fine," she waved off. "Buying a fake tree online was easy and safe, and I was able to make sure I got what I wanted. I'm totally good with this. In fact, I bought two of them. One for in here and one for the foyer." As an afterthought, she added, "Oh, I also bought these little scent sticks that will make the rooms smell like pine."

"Scent sticks?" I questioned skeptically.

"I hear your tone. Don't judge. I mean, yes—I would love to have a real tree, but I can make do for a year. And, as silly as it sounds, I'm kind of hoping that the pine smell from the sticks will draw attention away from why I don't have a real tree in the first place. This gilded cage can feel like a bit much sometimes," Krystina reasoned with a flip of her hand, motioning to the room around us.

Her tone was light, but I knew the truth behind her words. She looked up at me with a small smile of reassurance. She seemed happy—truly content to make do, scent sticks and all—and I didn't want to say or do anything to ruin that. She'd been through enough over the past couple of years. So instead, I pursed my lips and decided it was better not to push the issue of the tree any further.

Reaching for her, I pulled her tight to my chest once again. I just wished there was another way to keep Krystina and the baby we planned to have safe from harm. I hated that she was stuck in the house all the time —in a cage as she put it—and that it had been my decision to lock her up.

2

Alexander

I didn't particularly enjoy the holidays, but Krystina loved them. She usually did all the decorating, but I decided it wouldn't kill me to help her this year. Having already finished our dinner of Vivian's superb homemade squash ravioli in a delicious pine nut pesto, I worked alongside my wife to decorate the artificial pine. Krystina's playlist of upbeat Christmas music provided a festive backdrop as she regaled me with stories of Christmas past.

"When I was growing up, we had this Christmas Eve tradition. My stepfather and I always looked forward to it, but my mother..." she paused and tapped her finger against her chin as if she were trying to think of the right words. "Well, you know how difficult my mother can be at times—too serious, even at Christmas. She tolerated Frank's holiday shenanigans, but I loved every bit of the show he would put on."

"Show?" I asked with a raised brow. I had a hard time imagining Krystina's stepfather as a showman.

"Yeah, I guess you could call it that. Frank would get all decked out in this fancy Santa Claus costume. It was plush with shiny gold buttons. It looked so authentic, and no kid would dare question whether he was the real deal or not. He'd buy bags and bags of candy, and off we'd go to his car dealership where members of the local volunteer fire department would be waiting for us with their big red firetruck. That was the best part—riding in the truck. All the kids at school thought I was so cool for being allowed on a firetruck with *the* Santa Claus," she added with a laugh as she hung a silver ornament on one of the tree branches.

"As hard as I try, I can't picture Frank dressed as Santa."

"Oh, he did. He'd even stuff his suit, saying he needed to shake like a bowl full of jelly. Then he'd clamber to the top of the rig with his big ole' stuffed belly, and I would ride inside with my mother. The firefighters would blast Christmas music and let me pull the horn while 'Santa' threw candy to all the kids in low-income neighborhoods. It was so magical to me—the decorated truck, the music, and the excitement from all the kids. Afterward, Frank would invite the firefighters to the dealership where he'd serve them a catered gourmet meal right there in the massive showroom, complete with homemade figgy pudding. It was his way of saying thank you for their volunteer service to the community."

"I thought figgy pudding was just something made up for a song. It's a real thing?"

"It sure is. It's basically a molded pudding made from figs and other dried fruit. Frank's mother was British. Before she died, she would make it and bring it to Christmas Eve dinner. I never particularly cared for it. What about you?"

"Do I like figgy pudding? I just said I didn't even realize it was a real thing until—"

"No, no. Not figgy pudding. I meant traditions. Do you have any traditions from when you were...um, younger?" she finished hesitantly, knowing she may be asking a loaded question. I understood her caution. With my less-than-normal upbringing, anything was possible.

I shrugged indifferently.

"I've told you before, angel. Christmas was always just another day to me. With my dad constantly in between jobs, we had little money, but my mom did what she could for my sister and me. After everything happened with my mother and father, and Justine and I moved in with my grandparents, there were a few more gifts under the tree but not any traditions that I can remember."

It didn't surprise me that I couldn't recall any special Christmas traditions. I'd suppressed many of my childhood memories. It was a symptom of my PTSD which I was still trying to work through.

"Hmmm..." she contemplatively murmured as she stood back to observe the Christmas tree that was near completion. "Maybe I'll get some picture books and ask your mom if she remembers any tradition that you might have had. If there was one, maybe we could start it back up again—if not for you, then for her. It might make her happy."

An ache constricted in my chest as I thought about Helena, the woman who birthed me, residing in the west wing. The semi-private rooms, complete with a small kitchenette, were added onto the house specifically for her and the live-in nursing staff who cared for her. I hadn't visited her today, which was unusual. I typically stopped by at least once a day to check on her. Even though I made sure my mother had every amenity imaginable to keep her comfortable, the pain I felt every time I left her never seemed to ebb. While she had come to recognize the man I was now, she had no memory of me prior to our reintroduction four years ago—and she had no idea I was her son. She didn't even remember having any children, and telling her the truth would only confuse and upset her.

And all because of my father.

I gritted my teeth and my hands involuntarily flexed as I tried not to think about the physically and mentally abusive asshole. His death had allowed him to get off easy —but not before he reduced my mother to a shadow of her former self. The brain damage she'd suffered by his hands had been so severe that she struggled with even the most basic verbal and motor skills. Krystina's mention of picture books was another reminder of my mother's limited ability to communicate. Because she struggled to form words, her therapists showed us how to use pictures to converse with her. She had the mind of a small toddler trapped in an adult's body.

Nevertheless, Krystina had been good with my mother right from the very beginning. The way my mother's face would brighten whenever my wife walked into the room moved me in ways that were impossible to explain. Since my mother had no memory of my sister, Justine, or me, I doubted she would have any memory of a holiday tradition. If there were any traditions back then, Hale would most likely know about them. He'd been there through it all.

"You might have better luck asking Hale," I told Krystina.

"You might be onto something there. He was close

with your grandparents," she mused. "Maybe I'll get with him on it."

After packing up the empty ornament boxes, the two of us lugged them into the storage room in the basement. Once they were all neatly stowed away, Krystina and I returned to the living room and discovered that Vivian had made us mulled spiced cider. Two steaming mugs sat next to a plate of cinnamon biscotti. I heard a loud crackle and glanced toward the fireplace. Vivian had also added more wood to the fire.

A slow grin spread across my face, appreciating our housekeeper's ability to predict my desires—sometimes before even I knew what they were. It was no secret that decorating wasn't my thing, and as much as I always enjoyed my wife's holiday spirit, Vivian knew I would have other ideas for how Krystina and I should end the night—and she'd set the stage perfectly.

"I swear. I was literally just thinking about getting horizontal on the couch with you," I remarked. Stepping closer to Krystina, I snaked my arm around her waist. "Vivian is a mind reader."

"Yeah, she is," Krystina said quietly as her brows pushed together in a frown.

"What's wrong, angel?"

She didn't immediately answer and seemed to sink deeper into thought. When she eventually spoke, she couldn't mask the worry in her voice. "Once you think it's safe for people to come and go in the house again, I think we should consider hiring a part-time assistant for Vivian."

I pictured Vivian's deep smile lines and graying hair that she kept swept up into a bun. I nearly laughed when I thought about how our loyal housekeeper would react to such an idea. She was past retirement age, but I knew her well enough to know she was a perfectionist who thrived on staying busy.

"Vivian will never go for it," I replied. "She's way too particular. You know that. It's why I've trusted her with so much over the years."

"Maybe, but I think we should broach the subject with her. She does most of the cleaning and cooking for the household, including your mom's nursing staff. It's a lot for her. She's getting up there in age and should rest more. Tonight is a perfect example. It's after ten o'clock. She shouldn't be waiting on us at all hours as she does."

Sitting down on the curved Neiman Marcus sofa, I picked up a mug of hot cider and took a tentative sip of the hot liquid. While I'd preferred a nightcap with a bit more kick, I'd given up alcohol as a show of support for Krystina after she'd sworn off all alcohol and caffeine while we were trying to get pregnant. Giving up her favorite Washington State Riesling hadn't been too hard but switching to decaf was another story. Her penchant for coffee was something I would never understand. The love affair she had with caffeine ran deep.

Settling back, I crossed one ankle over my knee and

draped an arm over the back of the sofa. "Vivian likes doting on us—and she adores you. I dare you to try and tell her to stop. She won't listen."

Krystina sighed and bent to pick up her mug. "You're probably right, but I still think we should talk to her about taking on an assistant."

Walking over to the large floor-to-ceiling windows, she looked out into the dark night. At the moment, nothing but blackness could be seen, but I knew the view of the backyard to be breathtaking by day.

The house sat on a thirty-six-acre lot, of which five acres had been cleared to leave only a line of lush pines and tall maples dotting the landscape. They formed a natural path, following the gentle slope of the land to a large retention pond near the tree line. Krystina loved it out there in the summertime. On the weekends, when she wasn't lounging by our inground pool, she could often be found wandering the path around the pond. She had wanted to ice-skate on it during the winter months, but the unusually warm temperatures over the past few years meant thin ice—or sometimes no ice at all—and she hadn't been able to.

I studied my wife as she stared out into the black night. I couldn't help but notice the tension in her shoulders.

"Angel, come sit down," I told her. "You seem anxious."

"Do I?" she asked distractedly without looking at me.

"A little. If it makes you happy, I'll bring up the subject with Vivian this weekend."

Turning away from the window, Krystina came to sit down on the sofa. As she folded her legs under her, I wrapped one arm around her shoulders so she could curl into me.

A silence settled between us, one that seemed to stretch on for hours even though only about five minutes had passed. I loved the woman beside me in more ways than one, and despite the quiet, I knew my angel was deep in thought over something—and it had nothing to do with Vivian. As much as I wanted to dig into that brilliant and complex mind of hers, I decided not to poke the embers and stoke the flame. I had a suspicion about what she was thinking. If I was correct, as I almost always was when it came to her, it was best to stay silent and let her take the lead.

"Do you remember what today is?" she finally asked.

There it is.

Of course, I remembered what day it was. There was no way I would forget the third anniversary of her first miscarriage. The pregnancy came only a few short months after we were married. It hadn't been planned, but we were both excited by the news. When she lost the baby after only six weeks, it was a shocking blow.

"I remember," I replied with a slow nod. "That's why I came home from work early today. I didn't want you to be alone for too long."

I placed my hand on her thigh, lightly rubbing back and forth, as I waited for her to look at me. When she finally glanced up, tears glistened in her deep chocolate brown eyes but they didn't fall. She gave me a small smile instead.

"I appreciate that, Alex—more than you know. When I think about the past three years, I think about everything the doctor didn't prepare me for. I wish she had warned me about what was to come—even years later. Having a miscarriage isn't an event that's suddenly over. It's like running a goddamn marathon on a sad, agonizing road with nothing but emptiness waiting for you at the finish line."

I couldn't begin to name the things that stirred inside me. There was so much to say, yet so much that couldn't be said. So rather than analyze my feelings, I pushed them aside to focus on how she felt. I'd learned early on that sometimes all she needed was for me to hold her and listen while she grieved.

"Are you doing okay?"

"Surprisingly, yes," she said with a slight shrug. "Right now, I just miss normalcy. This time of year, I'd usually be shopping the Union Square Christmas Markets or browsing the 5th Avenue holiday window displays. But more than anything else, I miss seeing people. I didn't realize how much until today. It's lonely in this big house. I spoke to Ally via FaceTime this morning, but it wasn't the same. I wish I could see her in person—especially today, you know?"

Krystina had a special bond with her best friend, Allyson. While the two had always been close, they'd become even closer over the past three years. I attributed it to the fact that Allyson had been with Krystina when she had the first miscarriage. They'd been shopping when Krystina's severe cramping began, and Allyson had rushed her to the hospital. Unfortunately, I had been in Chicago on a business trip and couldn't get to her before the doctors broke the devastating news. I'd never forgive myself for not being there and had vowed to never be that far from my wife again.

"I realize you miss her, but you know why you can't see her in person. Ethan DeJames has Allyson all over the city doing photoshoots, many of which include a lot of people surrounding her. It's not safe for you to see her," I firmly reiterated.

My tone was stern enough for her to understand my resolve but not so harsh as to diminish her feelings. Allyson was a regular fixture in Krystina's life, even if I didn't like it. It wasn't that I had a problem with Allyson per se. I just didn't like it when she monopolized too much of my wife's time.

However, my feelings about that were now moot because of Krystina's isolation rules. We'd been over why she couldn't see her friend numerous times. Allyson was a photographer who was often on set with famous models and actors—all of whom came with a team of makeup artists, costume designers, and the like. I didn't need to remind Krystina of this any more than I wanted to go a round with her about why seeing Allyson in person was too risky. I knew she was frustrated, but I wasn't going to budge on this one. We'd already lost so much, and I'd do anything to prevent us from losing even more—not when there were things I could control to keep her safe.

Krystina squeezed her eyes closed and breathed deep, almost as if she was trying to find patience.

"I love that you're constantly looking out for me," she assured. "In fact, it was my first thought when I woke up this morning. I can't imagine how hard this pandemic must be for you. So much has been thrown into chaos and I know you're fighting to keep control wherever you can."

"No need to remind me, angel," I said sardonically.

"I try to keep that in mind every day. I know it's important to stay positive and not let the necessity for isolation get me down. That's not good for—" she stopped short, then sighed. "Negativity isn't good for anyone."

I frowned, wondering why she faltered before seeming to correct herself. I also noticed how she changed the direction of the conversation. She was clearly upset and missing her usual life, yet practically in the same breath, she was thanking me for looking out for her. It wasn't in my wife's nature to steer away from sensitive topics.

"What were you going to say?" I prompted, genuinely curious about what was moving the wheels in her head.

"Nothing," she said a little too hurriedly before continuing. "I will admit that I thought today was going to be rough. But then the Christmas tree was delivered, and I felt this shift inside me. I somehow knew I could get through the day just fine and that it was okay to move on from the past without feeling guilty. Everything happens for a reason, right? I hate to use that expression for this. It's so cliché and I can't think of a single reason why anyone should have to endure what we have. But I have to think our losses happened so we could experience something bigger. We have so much to look forward to, and I didn't want to spend today dwelling on what could have been."

"I think that's the best thing I've heard in a long time." I pressed a kiss to the top of her head. "We can't control bad things from happening, but we can control how we react to them. That's something Dr. Tumblin has been repeating to me for a while, and I think he's right."

She quirked up one eyebrow at me. "Really? What else has he said during your one-on-one sessions?"

I recalled the last video conference call I'd had with the psychiatrist my wife introduced me to a few years back. While I hadn't been a fan of the shrink at first, I'd come to appreciate the time spent with him. Dr. Tumblin helped me sort through the blackness in my soul and taught me to welcome life's small pleasures—and most of all, that I deserved to enjoy them without guilt. After the pandemic hit, his advice helped keep me grounded at a time when everything seemed to be spiraling out of control.

"He knows I'm worried about you and spends a lot of time making sure I don't confine you to our bedroom."

"I take that to mean he still doesn't know about your over-the-top efforts to keep me safe."

"I may have conveniently forgotten to mention it," I said with a wink, but she didn't seem to find anything amusing. Instead, she huffed out a frustrated sigh.

"Alex, really. We have a group session scheduled next week for the two of us. Therapy doesn't work if we keep lying to the doctor," she pointed out sardonically.

"Who's lying?"

"It's called lying by omission. Dr. Tumblin needs to know about your rules to protect me from a pandemic that doesn't even seem like a pandemic to much of the country anymore."

I narrowed my gaze, not liking this turn in the conversation.

"What do you mean it doesn't seem like a pandemic anymore?"

"Well, most people seem to have returned to semi-normal lives, Alex. I don't really keep up with the news anymore, but from what I've heard from others—"

"Krystina, don't," I interrupted. "You and I both know that you aren't most people."

She shook her head and sighed.

"I'm not trying to give you a hard time. I'm just voicing

frustrations. I don't want this to become a fight with us, which is why I think we should discuss it with Dr. Tumblin. I may get ornery about being cooped up from time to time, but I understand why you worry. In fact, this may be the one time your controlling nature has made me love you even more," she added with a laugh. "Sounds crazy, right? At the end of the day, I really just want to focus on what's ahead from now on."

I tightened my hold on her shoulders and leaned in to bury my face in her hair. Breathing deep, I inhaled the scent. Her lush locks smelled like strawberries and cream, and so very Krystina. With her, I sometimes wondered if things were too good to be true, and questioned whether the life I currently lived could possibly be real.

"Thank you for getting it, angel—for understanding why I need you to do this for me. I'd go crazy if anything were to ever happen to you. I love you so much."

"I love you, too," she murmured, then pressed her body closer to me. "And speaking of your controlling nature, have I told you lately how much that crazy, protective side of you turns me on?"

The corners of my mouth twitched, amused yet wondering where she was going with this at the same time.

"No, you have not."

Pulling away, she took the mug from my hand and placed it back on the table with hers. Then, grabbing the stereo remote, she changed the music from the upbeat

Harry Connick Jr. to something slower. The melodious voice of Sarah McLachlan filtered through the speakers, singing a song about a winter's night.

Turning to face me, she beckoned me with her finger. "Come here, husband."

3

Alexander

I raised an eyebrow at her sudden shift in mood.

"Giving me orders now, are you? You're always trying to top from the bottom," I teased with a little tsk.

However, I didn't waste time following her command, as I rather enjoyed it when Krystina played the temptress. Leaning in toward her outstretched finger, I nipped the tip of it with my teeth before pushing up her sleeve and trailing open-mouthed kisses up her arm. I lingered at the crook of her elbow just long enough to make her breath hitch before sliding the sleeve back into place and moving on. Tracing the curve of her collarbone with my fingertip, I inched closer so that I could nibble the line of her jaw.

Finding the hem of her oversized sweater, I skimmed a hand up her waist to brush the side of her lace-covered breast. She rewarded me with another sharp intake of breath as I bit the edge of her earlobe. I felt her shiver, igniting smoldering cinders of lust into red hot flames. Sliding my hand back down and around her hip, I tightly gripped her jean-clad ass. I wanted nothing more than to rip the restrictive denim from her body.

"I'm so fucking hard for you. Take your clothes off. I want you naked," I gruffly demanded.

A slow grin spread across my face when Krystina leaned back without hesitation and pulled her sweater over her head, revealing two perfectly shaped breasts cradled in a red lace bra. I loved it when she did as I asked without question. I couldn't wait to pin her arms above her head and feel her tight, submissive body beneath mine.

She shifted to stand in front of me, and her eyes flashed with desire as she made a show of slowly unbuttoning her jeans. Her hot gaze slid over me. The glow of the crackling fire behind her cast an orange halo around her body, making her look like my very own fire goddess. I nearly groaned.

"A striptease for your devil. I like it, angel," I murmured appreciatively. My gaze slid from her hands back up to her lush tits. The mere sight of them made me want to lose my mind, and I couldn't wait to see them bounce as I rode her. I noticed they looked a little fuller than usual, but I didn't dwell on the reason, knowing it was most likely due to the constant fluctuation of her hormones over the past few years. If anything, the added swell reminded me of everything she'd been through and the strength she had found to endure it. It only made me love her even more.

Reaching for her, I clasped my hands over hers, having this sudden need to undress her myself. I wanted to take my time and worship her—worship my wife, the woman I adored above all else.

Just as I began to slide down the zipper of her jeans, Krystina's cell phone started to ring. I frowned, looking to the coffee table where the incessant ringing was coming from. She twisted to pick up the phone and read the caller ID.

"It's Stone's Hope Women's Shelter," Krystina said with a note of confusion. "It's odd for them to call me this late. I should probably answer. It might be important."

Leaning back against the sofa cushions, I huffed out a frustrated breath and mumbled, "Make it quick."

Ignoring me, she slid her finger across the screen of the cell phone.

"Hello?" she answered.

I studied Krystina's face as she listened to the person on the other end of the line. Her expression grew more and more concerned with each passing minute.

"What is it?" I whispered.

She held up a finger, signaling for me to be patient,

then began speaking into the phone. "Claire, this isn't your fault. There was no way for you to have known. Just calm down. You've filed the police report, and there's nothing else to be done tonight. Let me think about this, and I'll call you tomorrow to discuss possible next steps. Everything will be okay."

I raised an eyebrow upon hearing the police were involved, but I couldn't say I was surprised. When managing a women's shelter, the police were often involved in things for various reasons.

About five minutes later, Krystina ended the call and turned to me.

"What was that all about?" I asked.

"It was Claire Stewart, the manager at Stone's Hope." She paused and brought her hands up to rub her temples, her distress evident. "A little over a year ago, I had convinced her to take a chance on one of the young mothers who had been a frequent flyer at the shelter. The mother's name was Hannah. She was constantly leaving her abusive boyfriend, only to go back to him because she couldn't support her daughter on her own."

I felt my jaw tighten, already knowing where this was going. The familiar tale of a woman in an abusive relationship was all too common. She may leave him, only to find herself returning for one reason or another. Sometimes it was because she believed the man had changed or had somehow flipped the blame onto themselves. Other times, it was simply because they were afraid. If there was a child involved, it was worse. Society wasn't designed with single working mothers in mind. It was the story of so many women—including my mother —and the reason I'd spearheaded the opening of the Stone's Hope Women's Shelter in coordination with The Stoneworks Foundation, my non-profit organization.

"Is the boyfriend the father of her daughter?"

"I'm not sure. I never asked," Krystina told me with a sad shake of her head. "There was just something about her story that tugged at my heart, so when I heard the shelter had a receptionist position open, I asked Claire if she would consider hiring her. She did, and Hannah has been working there ever since. We thought things were going well—until today."

"What happened?" I asked, although I wasn't entirely sure I wanted the answer.

Krystina pinched the bridge of her nose as if trying to squeeze away a headache. "I don't want to recap all of it now. It's nothing that can't wait until tomorrow. Besides, I think we were in the middle of something before my cell rang. What do you say we move what we started to upstairs in the bedroom?"

I smiled wickedly. While I was curious about what was happening, I was also irked by the disruption. I had been two minutes away from being balls deep in my sexy-as-hell wife, and I wasn't too happy that a late-night phone call had interrupted that.

"Angel, you read my mind."

A COLD GUST of air whisked across my naked body, jarring me awake. Feeling disoriented, I blinked in the darkness of the bedroom and tried to figure out why I was so cold.

Blankets. Where did the blankets go?

I groggily sat up and felt around in the bed, only to stop short when I heard a soft whimpering coming from beside me.

"Angel, what's wrong?" I whispered to Krystina. When she didn't respond, I could only assume that the whimper I'd heard was her mumbling in her sleep. She'd always been an active sleeper. Having entire conversations with herself and stealing all the blankets in the middle of the night was not a new occurrence.

Swinging my legs over the side of the bed, I got up and threw on a pair of boxer briefs, then made my way to the master bathroom. Flipping on the lights, I lowered the dimmer switch to make the light a bit more tolerable to my eyes. Standing in front of the long horizontal mirror hanging over the double-wide sink, I rubbed a hand over my day-old stubble.

I was annoyed that I'd been needlessly pulled from sleep, but I couldn't fault Krystina for it. She couldn't help dreaming any more than I could stop my nightmares from happening. She was fortunate not to be plagued with night terrors, but she had very vivid dreams. Some she remembered, and some she didn't.

More often than not, they were bizarre and, at times, even comical.

Turning on the faucet, I cupped my hands together and allowed them to fill with water. Then, after taking a quick drink, I closed the tap and began making my way out of the bathroom. My steps faltered when I heard Krystina's blood-curdling scream.

With my heart pounding in my ears, I rushed into the bedroom. The low light from the bathroom flooded the room, and I could see Krystina thrashing in the bed. Her chest rose and fell while her legs wildly kicked as if she were trying to throw off an imaginary villain.

I paused at the edge of the bed, unsure about what I should do. Experts believed you shouldn't wake a person from a nightmare because they may become confused or upset, potentially acting out physically and causing unintended injuries. It was a warning I'd given Krystina many times after she'd woken me from a terrible dream, as I never wanted to hurt her unintentionally.

"No! Please! No!" she cried out in the most terrified voice I'd ever heard from her lips. It was gut-wrenching.

Fuck what the experts say.

"Krystina, wake up!" I said firmly. When she didn't react, I bent to shake her by the shoulders. Her bare skin felt cold and clammy under my palms. "Come on, angel. Wake up. It's just a dream."

A moment later, her eyes snapped open and darted wildly around the room. I slid a hand down to her wrist and found her pounding pulse. Before I could assure her that everything was okay, she snatched her hand away and clutched her stomach. Still naked from our lovemaking earlier that evening, she looked down at her bare abdomen with a horrified expression. Moving quickly, she bolted into a sitting position, then shifted her body and appeared to be inspecting the sheets.

Blood. She's looking for blood.

Anguish ripped through my soul when I realized what she must have been dreaming about.

"Just a dream," she whispered, seeming to calm somewhat. It was almost as if she'd still been in her dream and had to convince herself she was back in waking life. Looking up at me, she repeated. "It was just a dream."

"Yes, angel. Just a dream." I ran my hand over the curve of her spine, noticing how bad she was trembling.

"I thought..." She trailed off. "Alex, it was awful. There were these dead, black hands coming up from the floor and trying to-to... I tried to get away, but—" She stopped short and choked on a sob.

"Shhh," I said, sliding in next to her and pulling her close. "You don't need to tell me about it. It wasn't real."

She clung to me as I tried to quiet her tears by stroking her softly. I kissed the top of her head, her cheeks, and her shoulders as if the press of my kisses would erase her demons. Seeing her so visibly shaken had gutted me, and I would do anything to make it all disappear.

I held her for a long while, not sure how much time

had passed before her body was finally free of the tremors. When she tilted her head up and brought her lips to mine, I inwardly sighed with relief.

"Are you feeling better?" I asked.

She didn't respond but shifted down to pepper my chest with kisses instead. Her hand slid down to the waistband of my boxers, feeling for the edge of the elastic. My cock reacted instantly—just as it always did with her —but I caught her hand before she could go any further and forced her head up to look at me. She stared back with pleading eyes.

"Alex, I need you."

"I'm right here, angel."

"No. I mean, I need you to make it disappear. Take me now. I need to know what's real."

I knew exactly how she was feeling. There was a heart-pounding rush of adrenaline that always came with a vivid nightmare. It didn't matter if the experience was nothing more than a figment of the imagination. The physical reaction in the body was real, and when that adrenaline was gone, all that was left was the memory of terror and a feeling of confusion. It was as if the mind couldn't process how to separate the dream from reality, and it needed something—anything—to stay grounded in truth.

So, I gave her exactly what she needed.

After shedding my boxers, I nudged her back until she was once again lying flat on the cool sheets. Positioning myself between her legs, I pinned her arms over her head and notched the head of my cock at her opening. Then I plunged deep, pumping hard and fast, chasing away the shadows of the night until her body hummed with the pleasure only I could give her.

4

Krystina

Rolling to the side, I slowly opened my eyes and allowed them to adjust to the light. Glancing at the clock, I saw it was just after six. The sheets beside me were slightly warm, and I could hear the shower running, signaling that Alexander was up and getting ready for work.

My mouth curved up when I heard him singing. I recognized *Winter Sound* by Of Monsters and Men almost instantly because it was a song that sparked many debates between Alexander and me. He insisted it was a Christmas song, while I didn't think it qualified as one just because it had the word 'winter' in it.

I softly hummed as he sang. Alexander had a magnificent voice, one that he didn't allow others to hear. I was the only lucky one. I smiled ruefully, thinking it was a shame that he would hide such a talent yet secretly pleased that it was reserved only for me. When it was just the two of us, he didn't try to hide his vulnerabilities anymore. Now, he let them flow freely.

My husband stepped from the master bathroom a few minutes later, wearing charcoal gray dress pants and a white button-down shirt. His matching dark gray suit jacket was slung over his arm as he knotted the burgundy tie at his neck. His gaze landed on me, and he flashed me one of those swoon-worthy smiles that I loved so much.

"Good morning, angel."

"Morning to you, handsome."

"How do you feel? Any more nightmares after you fell back asleep?"

"Not one," I assured.

"I guess I did my job then."

Walking over to the bed, he bent over to kiss me. It was a short kiss—tender and sweet—but still enough to make my toes curl. When he brushed the sheet aside to curve his palm over my breast, I crooned.

"Hmmm..." I breathed deep. He smelled of fresh water and woodsy cologne, an aphrodisiac to my senses.

Pulling back, he brushed a loose curl from my forehead, then returned to a standing position.

"Keep making noises like that, and it makes me want to skip work today," he told me, then grabbed my hand to press it to the front of his pants. His sapphire blue eyes darkened, and there was no mistaking the hard bulge I felt beneath his zipper. His need for me was an undeniable force, and I loved that I had that effect on him.

"Perhaps I should keep making those noises then," I teased, even though I was only half-joking.

"I wish I could. Trust me. I'd rather stay in bed with you all day than discuss quarterly revenues via teleconference with the board members of Stone Arena."

"Sounds incredibly boring."

"It is," he agreed as he slipped into his suit jacket. "I should be home on time tonight. If I can skate out early, I will."

Sitting on the edge of the bed, he brushed his fingertips down the side of my cheek. His gaze lingered on my mouth before he leaned down to give me another kiss.

I touched his face, softly moving my index finger along his jaw.

"I love you," I whispered.

Catching my finger, he pressed the tip to his lips. "I love you, too."

"I'll see you tonight."

After Alexander left the room, I flopped onto my back and extended my arms over my head to give in to a good stretch. My entire body felt absolutely delicious after last night. Even a terrible nightmare couldn't erase the heights Alexander had taken me to. As always, he'd wielded his authority over my body with flawless control. He had been on fire, taking me hard at first, then slowing to savor every inch of me. We didn't get to sleep until well after midnight, and when my nightmare pulled us both from our slumber, a quick round of fast and dirty sex was the only way to drive the demons away. My husband was insatiable—and he was a god in bed.

Still, echoes of what had haunted my sleep were hard to shake. Automatically, I brought both hands to my stomach and rubbed back and forth. The secret in my womb was still safe. No cold dead hands had taken it away from me.

It was just a dream. The baby is fine.

Guilt over keeping my pregnancy a secret from Alexander pressed down on my chest. When I'd awoken from the nightmare last night, I knew it was my subconscious punishing me for hiding the truth. The angel and devil on my shoulder had been at war pretty regularly as of late, and the guilt wasn't anything new. It had plagued me all hours of the day, but I'd always shoved it far into a corner where I would deal with it later.

There's nothing to feel guilty about. I'm doing the right thing.

It wasn't that I *wanted* to keep the baby a secret. On the contrary, I was over-the-moon ecstatic about the pregnancy and couldn't wait to tell everyone. However, I was also terrified.

Keeping the secret and carrying the burden of worry alone wasn't easy. I recalled that day in the master bathroom when I'd found out I was pregnant for the fourth time. My hands had wrapped like a vice around the little plastic stick as if it were my lifeline, equally frightened of either a positive or a negative result.

When I saw it was positive, I immediately felt like I'd stepped onto a tight rope, and I braced for the pain of loss to happen again. I was petrified of having that incredibly lonely feeling again; when I wanted to talk about it—to scream about it—but I had no safe place to yell when my husband was hurting just as much as I was.

My three miscarriages had eviscerated both Alexander and me, but I often wondered who took the loss of the third baby harder—him or me. I'd never seen him so distraught. Alexander and I drew on each other for strength, but I hadn't realized how much I pulled from him until I couldn't anymore. I was scared, and I needed him, yet every day, I had to remind myself of the reasons for remaining strong.

Tears began to sting the backs of my eyes, and I blinked them away as I recalled our agonizing losses. The first two pregnancies hadn't made it past six weeks. I'd barely known I was pregnant, but that didn't make it any less devastating. With the third, I'd been so sure I was in the clear. At eight weeks, I'd felt healthy and strong, and I had allowed myself to get excited once again. Alexander had fed off my enthusiastic energy. In some ways, it had been a transformative experience for him. I never thought I would hear my alpha male husband talk in a cooing voice to my stomach. He was downright giddy at times. It was charming and endearing, yet so out of character for him. It just made me love him even more.

But, in typical Alexander fashion, he tried to take control of the situation. As excited as he was about the baby, he was also a little neurotic. He had created spreadsheets to document every food I ate, craved, or abhorred. He'd wanted to know if I was tired or energetic and never failed to document the slightest change in my sex drive. So typical.

I never got mad about his obsessions, though. I loved how much he wanted to be a part of the process. The level of affection he'd displayed had cut through to a part of my soul I hadn't known existed.

When I lost the baby right before the twelve-week mark, he'd been crushed. Although he tried to stay strong for me, I saw the pain in those sapphire blue eyes that I loved so much, and I knew his heart had shattered into a million pieces. Now, I just didn't have it in me to give him false hopes. If I lost the baby again, of course, he would know. But perhaps if he didn't have all the buildup, the loss wouldn't hurt him so bad.

I still wasn't convinced I was doing the right thing by

keeping it a secret, but as of that moment, only my doctor knew I was pregnant. I couldn't tell anyone else— including Alexander—until I was through the most vulnerable weeks of the first trimester. I just couldn't bear to break his heart again.

I took one more look at the place Alexander had vacated before I awoke, and I felt my chest tighten. Climbing from the warm comforts of my blankets, I picked up my phone from the nightstand. After pulling up Alexander's contact information, I sent him a quick text.

TODAY 6:32 AM, ME:

I miss you already.

Setting my phone back down, I made my way to the bathroom and turned on the taps in the frameless glass shower. I stepped into the hot stream and took my time under the water. Cranking the temperature up, I braced my elbows against the Italian marble wall and indulged in thirty minutes of pure bliss under the rainfall showerhead.

When I was starting to prune, I climbed out and towel-dried my hair and body. Then, moving to my walk-in closet, I scanned my wardrobe for a minute before settling on a pair of black stretch pants and a knit funnel-neck sweater. If there was one advantage to working from home, it was that nobody cared or knew that my bottom half was almost always sporting a pair of leggings.

After applying a touch of makeup and throwing my

hair up in a semi-stylish messy bun, I made my way down to the kitchen. I wasn't surprised to find Vivian already there, as she was an early riser and was usually the first in the house to wake. She was seated on one of the barstools at the kitchen island, her reading glasses resting on the tip of her nose as she studied the crossword puzzle in front of her.

"Good morning, Vivian."

"Oh, good morning! I didn't hear you up and about. Can I make you a cup of coffee? Or what about breakfast? I can whip you up some eggs if you'd like. What shall it be?" She fired off the questions as she hurried off the stool.

My stomach roiled at Vivian's mention of eggs, and I nearly gagged. Masking my grimace, I flashed her a quick smile as I moved over to the coffee pot on the counter.

"No, no. Just relax. I'm fine. Please sit and finish your crossword puzzle. I can manage to scoop coffee grounds into a filter just fine on my own. Besides, I'm not very hungry this morning."

Especially not for eggs.

I could feel her eyes on my back as I scooped the decaf grounds into the basket, hoping she didn't notice my newfound disgust for sunny side up. While they used to be my favorite, I couldn't stomach them as of late. I just couldn't let her know, or she would tell Alexander. If that happened, questions were sure to follow, and I wasn't ready for that.

Unfortunately, keeping this little secret had been more challenging than I thought it would be, and not just because of the strange food aversions. My emotions were completely out of whack as well. I tended to go from laughing to crying in a split second. Just last week, I had wandered into the nursery bursting with joy, only to find myself overcome with tears about the three pregnancies I'd lost. When Alexander found me crying, I nearly broke down and told him I was pregnant again. I still wasn't sure how I maintained my resolve to keep it a secret.

My diet had been all over the board too. One minute I was starving, and the next, I was ready to vomit from just the smell of whatever food I'd craved just the day before. I'd caught Vivian giving me the side-eye a few times, but if she suspected anything, she didn't let on. I wasn't new to the woes that came with the first trimester. I'd already decided that the person who dubbed the nausea I constantly experienced as morning sickness was a liar. It should have been called all-day sickness. After all, this was my fourth time experiencing it, so I knew a thing or two about it—and I deserved an Emmy for the way I managed to hide it from Alexander. While I never actually vomited, the constant rolling in my stomach was trying. The only thing that made it tolerable was knowing that I didn't have much longer to go before the nausea should start to subside. Until then, I needed to stick to the plan. Alexander would know about our baby soon enough.

I sidestepped to the refrigerator to retrieve the coffee

creamer, resisting the urge to place my hand on my stomach. It was an instinct that seemed to happen whenever I was pregnant. After adding a dollop of cream and a pinch of sugar, I retreated to the confines of my office, where I could escape Vivian's watchful eye.

5

Krystina

With my feet up on the corner of my desk, I swallowed the last dregs of my coffee as I clicked through emails. There was an email from Sheldon Tremaine at Beaumont Jewelers letting me know that my Christmas present for Alexander was ready to ship. Not only was Sheldon a client of mine, but Alexander and I were also customers of his. He had designed several pieces of jewelry for me, including the triskelion necklace Alexander had given me, and I knew he was a master at his craft. I could count on him to deliver exactly what I wanted.

I smiled to myself, already feeling excited about the

custom-made gift for my husband. It was hard finding a gift for a man who already had everything, and the ornate twenty-four-carat gold design was precisely what I'd been looking for.

I continued going through the emails, the repetitive sound of my finger pressing on the mouse the only thing that could be heard in the quiet house. The silence was almost deafening, and a feeling of loneliness washed over me.

When I still reported to my office on the thirty-seventh floor at Cornerstone Tower, Alexander had only been an elevator ride away. We'd have lunch together and even sneak in a quickie here and there. Now it felt like Alexander was slipping away from me. Perhaps it was because I'd been seeing him less. With him always an hour away in the city, I was constantly left home alone. Well, I wasn't technically alone, but it felt like that whenever I wasn't near him. He was my addiction, and I needed him like the air I breathed.

Pushing away the feeling of loneliness, I finished the arduous task of filing my emails. I flagged the ones that needed responses and trashed the junk messages. Despite the economic problems in the city, business was going well, and I had clients booked through the end of next year. I knew how fortunate I was during these tumultuous times and never failed to appreciate it.

As I considered all those who'd been struggling, I thought about the call I received last night from Claire

Stewart. The office manager at Stone's Hope was reliable and competent. She was known to have a level head even under the most trying circumstances, so it was a bit jarring when she called me in a panic. Still, I understood why she was so upset.

When Claire had gone in to close the November accounting books, she found the operating account had been wiped clean. After spending the entire day trying to get answers from the bank about where the money went, she'd discovered a thirty-two thousand dollar transfer was made. The money had been transferred to an account under the name of Hannah Wallace, the single mother Stone's Hope had hired over a year ago. And now, Hannah was missing.

Claire had followed the appropriate steps. She was in regular contact with the bank and had called the police to file a report. However, she hadn't even thought about the December operating budget in all her worrying about finding the money. Once she realized the only cash the shelter had left were the funds raised for Christmas, she panicked because that money was slated to buy gifts and host a small holiday party for the mothers and children staying at the shelter. It was why she had called me late last night. Claire couldn't stomach the idea of using that money to cover the December operating expenses, and she was hoping I'd be able to give her an alternate solution.

Before I could do that, I needed to call Stephen

Kinsley, Alexander's trusted friend and lawyer. He managed Alexander's legal matters, including all things related to The Stoneworks Foundation, the parent organization of Stone's Hope Women's Shelter. If anyone would know what to do about all of this, he would. Picking up the phone, I dialed his number.

"Stephen, hi. It's Krystina," I said after his secretary put me through to him.

"Krystina! It's been a while. To what do I owe the pleasure?"

"We've got a problem. I haven't filled Alexander in on the details yet, but since he usually lets Justine and me handle everything with the women's shelter, I figured I would just get with you directly." I explained the situation to Stephen while he listened quietly. When I was through, I heard him sigh.

"This is a tough one, Krystina. Fortunately, theft from a charity is rare, but it happens more frequently during tough economic times like we are experiencing now. Claire did the right thing by reporting the misappropriations to the police. If she didn't, it would raise questions if the Attorney General ever decided to investigate."

My brows arched in alarm. "The Attorney General?"

"Yeah. Theft from a non-profit isn't like theft from a normal business entity. Non-profits have to follow a whole different set of rules. I'll have to get with a forensic accountant to deep dive into the books to ensure there isn't more missing money. What Hannah did here, assuming she's guilty, is larceny, but she also might have been skimming long before this happened."

My stomach dropped.

"Oh, no. I hadn't even considered that. Let's hope not."

"At some point, the IRS will most likely need to be involved, but I'm not going to jump the gun on that until we know exactly what we are dealing with. Is Claire at the shelter now?" Stephen asked.

"She should be."

"Good. I'll send one of my investigators to talk to her later today or tomorrow so we can get the ball rolling. Then, we'll go from there."

"Thanks, Stephen. I appreciate the help. In the meantime, can we move money from another area of the Foundation to cover the December operating costs at Stone's Hope? This way, we don't have to use the money set aside in savings for Christmas."

"Unfortunately, no. A transaction like that isn't allowed. Stone's Hope is a subsidiary of The Stoneworks Foundation, but operates under a different tax ID."

I frowned in confusion. "I don't understand. How does that impact our ability to move money?"

"The Foundation can't just transfer that dollar amount to an outside entity without the approval of the Attorney General or the court. Transferring assets that impact a charity's ability to operate takes time. If we don't follow the proper procedures, it could put the entire Foundation at risk. I know you don't want to, but you're going to have to use the Christmas funds to cover the operating costs so that you don't default on the bills. I'm sorry I don't have a better answer for you."

My stomach sank with a feeling of hopelessness. "That's okay. Keep me updated on the investigation. Thanks again for your help, Stephen."

"Anytime."

I ended the call, sat back in the chair, and began to drum my fingernails on the desk. The shelter was personal to Alexander—so personal that when he trusted me enough to oversee the regular operations at Stone's Hope, it had been one of the greatest honors of my life. For me, it was a different kind of declaration of his love. There had to be something I could do, but I didn't know what.

Sighing, I turned back to my computer. I would have to think more about the problems at the shelter later. I currently had emails that I needed to finish sorting and a holiday ad blitz to roll out for Beaumont Jewelers. Turning back to my computer, I got to work on the pending deadlines.

As I neared lunchtime, I stood over a small conference table studying a pile of design mockups sent over by Clive, the Lead Marketing Coordinator at Turning Stone Advertising. I placed the more eye-catching ads on A-framed easels. *The Best of Pentatonix Christmas* played quietly in the background to create a bit of noise in the otherwise silent house. When my stomach began to rumble, I knew it was time to take a break. Pregnancy hunger pains were no joke, and I needed to tend to them immediately.

Placing my hand on my stomach, I looked down and whispered, "Are you getting hungry, little one? Don't worry. Just let mommy clean up here, then I'll get you some lunch."

I began to shuffle the designs back into a pile but was interrupted when my cellphone rang. It was Alexander making his usual mid-day check-in.

"Hey, you," I said upon answering.

"Hey, yourself. How's my angel doing today?" he asked in that voice that was just as disarming as his looks.

"I'm a little tired. Somebody kept me up late," I reminded him.

"I didn't hear any complaints coming from your lips. Just a lot of 'Oh, Alex' and—"

"Okay, okay!" I interrupted. "No need to repeat it!"

Alexander laughed but then quickly sobered. "I talked to Stephen today. I just hung up with him, actually."

"Did he tell you what's going on at Stone's Hope?"

"He did. Have you spoken anymore to Claire about it today?"

"No. I haven't called her yet because I don't know what to say."

"There are too many legal concerns. It's best if you let Stephen handle it," Alexander advised. "Ultimately, I don't know what that woman, Hannah, was thinking when she transferred all that money. She had to have known she'd be caught. It's such a shame."

"I know. It breaks my heart to think about it. I'm trying to focus on this ad campaign, but I haven't been able to get the situation with Stone's Hope out of my head all morning. There must be something I can do, but with all the non-profit rules and regulations, I keep coming up empty-handed. It's going to be hard feeling happy about Christmas this year when so many will have nothing. I just keep picturing the faces of the little ones at the shelter. They've all been through so much, and I can't imagine them not having a Christmas."

"Krystina, don't beat yourself up over this. We'll think of something."

"I should at least get some toys for the kids. Stephen only discussed money, and never mentioned toy donations. Maybe we could do something like Frank did when I was little. If I could convince you or Hale to dress as Santa, we could pop into the shelter and surprise them all."

"Absolutely not," he stated firmly.

"Okay, forget the Santa thing. Maybe—"

"It's not about who's dressing up as Santa, although the idea of me doing any such thing is ludicrous. This is about you not leaving the house."

"But, Alex—"

"I'm not arguing about it. If you want to buy toys, fine.

Order them online and have them delivered. But you know why you can't go to the shelter."

"That's so impersonal," I muttered. "Never mind. Forget I even mentioned it."

I knew I would lose if I continued to push. After more than a year of Alexander treating me like a fragile china doll, I should have predicted this reaction from him. He was pushing me to my limit, and I knew it was starting to impact our relationship. It was only a matter of time before my frustrations won out. Thankfully, our therapy session with Dr. Tumblin was only a few days away and I committed right then to bring this up with him—whether Alexander wanted me to or not.

"Angel, I'm just trying to keep you safe," Alexander reiterated.

"I know," I responded quietly.

"Do you remember what you said last night about staying positive and focusing on the future?"

"Yes."

"Keep that mindset. A positive mind can only help as we create our tiny human. Who knows? Maybe we did it last night."

As if his words had summoned them, the angel and devil on my shoulders decided to rear their annoying little faces. The angel chastised me, her nose growing long like Pinocchio's, while the devil cheered me on for being such a fabulous liar.

Not much longer to wait. I'll tell him soon.

"Yeah, maybe," was my only reply.

"Alright, if all is okay, I've got to be going. I need to prep for a conference call scheduled with Kinsley Properties. I shouldn't be home too late today. I hope to leave the office by four and be home by five. Call me if you need anything in the meantime."

"Will do."

"I love you, angel."

"Love you, too. I'll see you when you get home."

As I placed my phone back on my desk, my stomach began to rumble again, reminding me that I still hadn't gotten lunch. I pushed away the pang of guilt I felt over my lie and absently rubbed a hand over the impatient little bundle of joy growing inside of me.

"Your daddy can be crazy and overbearing, but I still can't wait to tell him about you," I whispered, then hurried to the kitchen to grab us a bite to eat.

6

Krystina

"I am not discussing this!" Alexander boomed, his voice echoing off the tall ceilings in his home office. His eyes angrily flashed as he stood up and began to pace. His five o'clock shadow seemed to add a dangerous edge to his already savage mood.

We were more than halfway through our monthly therapy session with Dr. Tumblin, and Alexander, as usual, was trying to control the direction of the conversation. But unfortunately, I'd thrown him for a loop when I brought up the compulsory quarantine that he'd imposed on me for the past twelve months. Dr. Tumblin wanted to discuss it further, but my husband wasn't having it.

Dr. Tumblin sat unperturbed, watching us through the laptop computer screen sitting on a small round table before me. I sighed and leaned back in my chair. I knew Alexander would be angry with me for telling the psychiatrist about my isolation, even though the whole reason we had these sessions was to help keep Alexander's controlling nature in check. While we usually functioned just fine as a couple, we both knew how easily his domineering nature could take over our lives. Navigating his need for control with my need for independence could sometimes be a tricky balancing act.

"Alex, you can't avoid this," Dr. Tumblin said patiently.

"Can't I?" Alexander shot back testily.

"Look, Alex. Krystina pushed very hard to get you to open up to me—to be truthful during our sessions. We've made great progress, and you've both said you were happier as a couple because of it. Why are you choosing to shut down after all this time? Tell me what's going on."

"It's nothing," Alexander bit out.

Turning in my chair, I glanced back at my husband to see him shove his hands through his dark waves. He was pacing like a trapped animal looking for an escape and I was reminded of why I never put my foot down about his asinine rules in the first place. When he got like this, there was no reasoning with him. He was too stubborn.

Alexander had always gone above and beyond to give

me anything I could ever want. But the thing I'd wanted most was to have everything back to normal. I'd wanted my life back—people, restaurants, shopping, and parties. It sounded superficial, but the human element to those things made it so much more. But then I'd found out that I was pregnant, and all the speeches I'd planned in front of the mirror about why I shouldn't be quarantined had been thrown out the window. Now, just thinking about desiring any of those things made me feel incredibly selfish. It didn't matter how isolated I felt. This wasn't just about me anymore. I had a baby to think about too, but that didn't mean I wasn't torn. I wanted normalcy, but I also wanted the safety Alexander demanded.

"Alex, please sit down," I said. "There's no reason to be angry. I understand why you have these rules. I wouldn't have followed them if I didn't mostly agree with you. I just think the rules can be a bit extreme—especially with Christmas right around the corner. I've told you this before, but you didn't want to listen. I thought Dr. Tumblin could help us work through it. It's not just about me either. I mean, the hoops you make Vivian and Hale jump through are a bit over the top, too."

"Krystina..." Alexander trailed off, but his warning tone was unmistakable.

"What about Vivian and Hale?" Dr. Tumblin asked.

"Our staff has been impacted by this as well. They've had to make major adjustments," I explained. "Even the most basic things, such as buying groceries, has to be done online with curb-side pickup. Vivian detests doing anything that requires technology, so I usually place the grocery order for her. I know she doesn't like it but will never complain. Hale never complains either. But at least those two get to leave the house on occasion. I feel bad for Alex's mothers' nursing staff. They can't leave at all."

"Alex, have you made all of these rules just to keep Krystina safe from the pandemic?"

"Yes," Alexander said through gritted teeth.

"If you've been this concerned, why haven't you mentioned any of this to me before now?" Dr. Tumblin asked.

"Because I didn't need you to tell me that I was being irrational," Alexander barked.

"Is that how you feel? Irrational?" Dr. Tumblin prodded. Alexander didn't respond. Instead, he resumed his silent pacing.

Despite his surly expression, I couldn't help but notice the way he could effortlessly own the room. His tall frame commanded power and radiated prestige. I wondered if a day would ever come when I would tire of watching him. Even when he was irritated, he was impossibly gorgeous, and I couldn't help the magnetic pull I felt whenever I was near him. He was the other half of my soul, and I wouldn't be able to survive without him.

Alexander shoved a hand through his dark hair that was already unruly from the way he'd been running his fingers through it in frustration. His sapphire eyes swirled with conflicted emotion, and his lips were drawn into a grim line. It was as if he was torn—knowing I was right about how he'd forced me into isolation but also unwilling to change his position on the matter.

I fought the urge to go to him, wanting to apologize for bringing any of this up. After all, it wasn't that big of an issue. But then again, maybe it was. Alexander and I had been through similar things before, and it was why we decided to keep our monthly couple's therapy sessions with Dr. Tumblin. Surprisingly, it had been Alexander's idea. He'd said that he didn't need the psychiatrist to help him work through his past issues any longer but admitted that he still had significant control issues. He worried that his need to control everything in his life—including me— could be detrimental to our relationship, and he wanted Dr. Tumblin to point out his more irrational urges. Up until recently, that had worked, and Alexander and I spent the past four years in relative harmony.

But now, everything had changed.

When the world shut down, everything seemed to spiral out of control. A global threat just may have been the worst thing to happen to someone with Alexander's controlling personality. During my efforts to ease his worries, I'd went along with every one of his wishes until I eventually began to feel powerless. I hated feeling that way, and I knew it would inevitably lead to problems in our marriage—which was precisely why I told Dr. Tumblin about everything today. He was the one person who understood Alexander as I did, and I knew he'd be able to help us adapt to our ever-changing environment. While Alexander and I were still the same couple who sat before Dr. Tumblin on countless occasions before, the world was different, and the usual strategies might not apply.

I almost said as much, but I hesitated. At that moment, Alexander was too keyed up and he needed to see this on his own. Nobody could force him. Pushing him may only make a bad situation worse, so I waited for Dr. Tumblin to take the lead.

After another minute of waiting for Alexander to respond, Dr. Tumblin finally spoke.

"Alex, much of the world has returned to a relatively normal life. Yes, there are precautions that need to be taken, but nothing unreasonable. Why don't you trust Krystina to be careful?"

"You don't understand, Doc. It's not about whether I trust her. It's about my dreams—or rather, my nightmares," Alexander said bitterly. "Do you remember back to about eighteen months ago, when I told you I was no longer having reoccurring nightmares about my past?"

"I do," Dr. Tumblin replied.

My brows pushed together in thought, wondering where Alexander was going with this.

"The nightmares didn't stop—they just changed," Alexander explained.

"What do you mean?" Dr. Tumblin asked.

I was genuinely confused. I hadn't woken up to my husband's thrashing in bed in so long. If he was still suffering nightmares, I'd been completely unaware.

Alexander came to sit back down in the chair next to me. He glanced at me for a moment, then turned his attention to the computer screen. Focusing all his attention on Dr. Tumblin, his deep blue eyes seemed to plead for understanding.

"The nightmares came to me by day. They didn't wake me from sleep—they kept me from sleep," Alexander told him. Taking my hand, he squeezed it to let me know he was addressing me as well. "The nightmare happened every time I heard an ambulance siren or heard about the climbing death toll on the news. Any reports about the increased risks to pregnant women just about sent me over the edge. I couldn't block out visions of Krystina in a hospital bed, on a ventilator, or worse. The images were far more terrible than any nightmare could ever hope to be. They only subsided after Krystina agreed to isolation. So, I don't care who thinks my rules are extreme. There's still a threat. We've already lost so much, and I'll do whatever it is I have to do to keep my visions from coming to fruition."

"Alex, much of the world feels exactly as you do. Unfortunately, you're not alone in this," Dr. Tumblin said with conviction.

"I can value your assurances almost as much as I appreciate the time spent on our sessions. Your words matter," Alexander said earnestly. "You've helped me sort through the blackness in my soul. But this... this is different. You won't be able to convince me to see this differently. Krystina's well-being and safety are, and always will be, my number one priority."

"Thank you for your honesty," Dr. Tumblin said. "As I've always said, I can't help either of you if you aren't being truthful. I just wish you hadn't kept this from me for so long."

A pang of guilt pierced my heart because Alexander wasn't the only one keeping a secret from the psychiatrist —nor was it the first time we were in this situation. Alexander's need for privacy always took precedence, so there was a lot that Dr. Tumblin didn't know about us. I wasn't looking forward to the microscope that he was sure to turn on me once he found out I was pregnant and had been hiding it for months.

"Whether you knew about Krystina's isolation or not wouldn't have changed my decision," Alexander added. "Especially when you consider that we are trying to get pregnant."

"I believe this is something we are going to have to dig deeper into during our one-on-one sessions, Alex. However, since you mentioned trying to get pregnant again, I'd like to ask both of you if Alexander's deep concern about safety has impacted any other areas of your life."

I shifted my gaze from the computer screen to

Alexander. His gaze remained impassive, and I wondered if he would get upset if I brought up my next topic of concern—the way he'd changed when we were together intimately. My usually dominant husband had noticeably altered certain activities, almost as if he thought I was a fragile little bird that could be damaged in too strong of a breeze. Our days of bondage and discipline seemed to be a thing of the past—or at least the bondage part was.

"Well," I began hesitantly, unsure if this was the right setting for this topic. "There is one thing. It's not a huge concern, but I think..."

When I trailed off, Alexander looked at me curiously while Dr. Tumblin continued to stare with his seemingly unending well of patience.

"Go on," Alexander prompted.

My hands fidgeted in my lap, doubting whether I should continue. Alexander had gotten upset with me once before for mentioning his BDSM lifestyle to Dr. Tumblin, but that was years ago, and it had nothing to do with us as a couple and everything to do with Alexander's past. Now, sex was never a topic discussed in our therapy sessions. We didn't need to because it was the one area that never had any problems—until recently, that is.

When Alexander and I first got together, I knew very little about BDSM. He'd given me a crash course, and while we didn't practice the more extreme aspects of it, I'd come to enjoy what we did together. He was the master of kink and could take me to heights I never thought imaginable. When we'd built this house together, Alexander had included a playroom accessible only through a secret movable bookcase in our bedroom. Complete with shackles and a plethora of other toys, we'd used the room regularly, but it had been close to a year since Alexander had last sent me there.

At first, I thought it was because I'd done something wrong. However, as the months continued to pass, I began to think there was a deeper reason for not using the playroom. I just wasn't sure what it could be.

I looked up to meet Alexander's piercing blue gaze. I'd already pushed my husband to the edge of a precipice by challenging my isolation. I wasn't sure if talking about our sex life would send him over the edge. However, before I was forced to decide, an idea came to mind.

"Dr. Tumblin, would you mind if I muted us for one moment?"

"Oh. Um, sure," he replied, sounding somewhat surprised.

It didn't matter what his reply was. I wouldn't have listened if he said no and was already leaning forward to mute the microphone on our video conference call.

Thank God for modern technology.

Once the little icon had a red slash through it to signal that the mic had been successfully muted, I turned to Alexander.

"It's been a year since we last used the playroom," I

blurted out. "Why haven't you wanted to use it? Have I done something wrong?"

Alexander's eyes widened as his shock registered. "I'm sorry. What?"

"The playroom. Why haven't you brought me there lately?"

"Isn't it obvious?" he asked.

"Well, no. If it were, I wouldn't be asking."

"First of all, you were right to mute the computer, Krystina. Our sex life will never be any of Dr. Tumblin's business."

"I figured as much. That's why I did it," I said with a shrug and looked down at my hands. Despite my best efforts, they were fidgeting in my lap again. I clamped my palms together, focusing my attention on the wood graining of the table. After nearly four years of marriage, I knew I shouldn't be nervous about having this conversation. But for some reason, I was.

"Angel, what we do in the playroom can be taxing on the body. I don't want you doing anything too strenuous anymore, especially after your last miscarriage," he said, then paused to pinch the bridge of his nose. When he trained his eyes on me once again, those gorgeous, expressive blues were full of turmoil and guilt. "The playroom is a hard limit for me for the immediate future. I just can't risk it. What happened the night before you miscarried...it was my fault...I...I shouldn't have..."

My eyes widened as he faltered trying to explain. A

horrible understanding crept in. He didn't even need to finish the sentence. I knew what he was thinking.

The night before I'd lost our third baby, Alexander and I had been in the playroom. I remembered it clearly because it was the last time that we used the room. Goosebumps raced down my spine, igniting an instant fire in my belly as I recalled the way I'd been restrained face-first against the wall with my hands shackled above my head. Alexander had been merciless with the flogger, slowly working me over and bringing me to the brink of ecstasy over and over again.

The cracking sound against my skin echoed in my mind. I'd felt glorious, but I couldn't ignore what Alexander just said about not wanting me to do anything too strenuous. I had been straining that night, pulling against the binding restraints as I succumbed to the pleasures only my husband could bring me.

Now I knew why Alexander seemed to take the loss of our third baby so much harder. He blamed himself for it. It shattered me to realize he'd been carrying that guilt around this entire time.

No. No. No. It wasn't his fault. It was nobody's fault.

I wanted to scream the words but only managed to shake my head in denial before glancing back at the computer screen. Dr. Tumblin was waiting with a curious expression. Leaning in, I unmuted the mic.

"Dr. Tumblin, we're all set for now," I said. "Alex and I need to talk about something. We only have about five minutes left in our session anyway. Can we pick this back up next month?"

"Sure, I guess. Is everything okay, Krystina? You look a bit alarmed."

"Everything is fine. Like I said," I paused to give a meaningful look at Alexander. "We have something to talk about, and I think it's best if we go at it ourselves."

"Alright," Dr. Tumblin conceded, albeit reluctantly. "If you need anything, you know how to reach me."

"Thank you," I said with a short nod. Alexander did the same, and I ended the video chat. Then, taking his hand, I led him over to the small leather loveseat on the opposite side of the office. I sat down, then patted the area next to me.

Alex moved to sit beside me, then reached up to cup my cheek and said, "Angel, I—"

"Shhh. It's my turn to talk." I shushed him by bringing a finger to his lips. "What happened... it wasn't your fault. You cannot blame yourself. I won't have it."

Taking my finger from his lips, he began to kiss it softly while staring intently at me. The anguish in his eyes nearly gutted me.

"Krystina, I was the one who fastened those leather cuffs to your wrists. I didn't consider the risks, and you were too aroused at that moment to be thinking clearly. What if—"

"What if nothing," I said, effectively cutting him off again by pressing my mouth to his.

Our lips moved slowly as Alexander fisted his hands in my hair. He drew me closer to him, deepening the kiss. I wanted the languid movement of our lips and the gentle swipes of my tongue to show him how much I irrevocably trusted him and could never blame him for our loss.

He pressed his mouth harder to mine, almost as if he were signaling that he understood. Our hands roamed in tender caresses of exploration over backs and shoulders, up and down arms, and moving to cup each other's faces. I moaned against him as the intensity of what flowed between us sent shockwaves through my system. When we finally broke apart, our breathing was ragged.

"You're so goddamn beautiful," he whispered. Emotion was heavy in his voice as he stared intently into my eyes. "I wouldn't survive if something happened to you —whether it be by my hands in the playroom or this godforsaken virus. So, please. Let me do what I need to do to keep you safe, angel."

The intensity of his words nearly leveled me, and my throat clogged with emotion. Burying his face into my neck, he breathed deep, then began peppering kisses along my jawline. I angled my head, inviting him to take more and relishing the feel of his lips as they traveled down my neck.

"I need you, Alex. Take me. Right here," I breathed.

Pulling back, he looked into my eyes. I was able to see the visible shift in his demeanor when those sapphire blues darkened with unfulfilled promises.

Not wasting a moment, he nudged me back until I was horizontal on the loveseat, then gripped the waistband of my yoga pants with both hands. Yanking both the pants and my underwear down over my hips, he shimmied them over my thighs and calves until my bottom half was completely bare.

His gaze was dark and primal as he moved to place open-mouthed kisses up my legs, stopping just before he reached the apex of my thighs. Parting them slightly, he slid one finger along my waiting slit.

"Oh!" I gasped as he softly grazed the pulsating bundle of nerves.

"My angel is already wet. Good," he said appreciatively.

Then, without warning, he stood, bringing me with him by lifting me until my legs were scissored around his hips. There was no denying the hardness of his erection straining through his pants and against my naked heat. He wanted this as much as I did.

Moving me to the empty wall next to the sofa, he pressed me up against it. His eyes never left mine the entire time, reminding me of the eternal connection we shared. His gaze was full of fire and lust yet transfixed with reverent intensity.

"Tighten your legs around me and hang on, angel."

Doing as he asked, I squeezed my legs around his hips and gripped his hard biceps with my hands. I felt his rippled muscles bunch beneath his black cotton t-shirt as he worked to unfasten his belt and the fly to his jeans. A moment later, I heard a thud that signaled his pants had fallen to the floor. Wrapping one arm tightly around my waist, he used his free hand to notch the throbbing tip of his cock to my slick entrance.

"Are you ready for me, baby?" he asked in a guttural tone.

"Always."

In one quick thrust, he plunged his shaft through my tight clasp until he was completely sheathed. I let out a groan of pleasure, fully surrendering to every sensation only Alexander could make me feel. He impaled me over and over again until my moans turned into borderline screams.

When I finally came, the rushing release was all-consuming. But Alexander didn't stop there. He continued to sink deeper and harder until I could feel nothing but the delicious pulsing of his seed bursting forth.

7

Alexander

"Riverside Grille too? That's the second tenant we've lost this week," I said irritably to Bryan, even though I knew none of this was my accountant's fault.

Bryan didn't deserve my ire, but I didn't care. The economic times we lived in coupled with my easily irritable state was a bad combination. It had been four days since the therapy session with Dr. Tumblin, and I'd been feeling edgy ever since. I didn't like the way Krystina was pushing me and it seemed as if even the littlest thing had the ability to piss me off.

"You could always cut out Christmas bonuses for the staff to make up for the lost revenue," Bryan replied.

"I've already said that wasn't an option," I barked.

"I think they would understand if—"

"Bryan, I said it wasn't an option. Think of something else."

"I've considered what Riverside's current income flow might look like. The ratios for takeout business versus indoor dining are different for each restaurant, but they might be able to handle a monthly payment plan option to get caught up on past due rent," he suggested.

"I don't think that will be realistic. Restaurants were hit the hardest, and they still aren't seeing the customer flow they once had. People are finally just starting to come back to the city. You should know that after everything Matteo has said," I pointed out, reminding him of the many struggles my best friend, Matteo Donati, had gone through with his restaurant, Krystina's Place. "How many months of rent does Riverside owe?"

I heard some shuffling of papers before Bryan responded, "Eight months."

Jesus.

That was the most any restaurant tenant of mine was behind in rent. While I didn't have any particular loyalty to the family-owned restaurant, I felt obliged to help them out for some reason.

"Eight months isn't going to break the bank. If there's a chance that they can stay in business, erase the debt and let them start fresh. I can't stomach to see another restaurant in Manhattan close."

"Whoa. You want to erase it completely?" Bryan asked incredulously. "We're still dealing with the loss of revenue at Stone Arena. We've only just started booking large events again, and then there's—"

"Don't argue with me on this," I stated firmly. "Erase the debt, and when you report back, I want to hear they decided not to close their doors."

Without giving him a chance to protest further, I hit the end call button on the desktop phone. Then, not skipping a beat, I pressed the intercom button for my assistant.

"Laura," I said into the speaker.

"Yes, Mr. Stone."

"Where are we on the vacant Stone Enterprise properties? Have we published the interior photos of them and started advertising?"

"That's ready to go, sir. Turning Stone Advertising is set to handle that after the first of the year."

"Good, good. I trust Krystina will do a fantastic job with it. Also, I've decided to buy the staff lunch today from Riverside Grille. Find out what they want and charge the order to the operating account."

"Yes, sir."

"Oh, and make sure they don't congregate when the food arrives," I added. "Protocols are still in place, which includes wearing their masks when they aren't at their desks."

"I'll remind them," Laura assured.

The staff knew my concerns about keeping Krystina safe, but it didn't hurt to reinforce the rules now and then. I was a stickler for precautions, but sometimes I felt like it wasn't enough—especially when I knew every single one of them thought I was exaggerating the need for them. Only half of the staff at Stone Enterprise reported to the office, while the other half still worked remotely. Personally, I didn't have the luxury of working from home, or else I would. Stone Enterprise was just too big of an entity for me to manage off-premises. Because of that, strict in-house rules with frequent reminders would have to suffice.

Leaning back in my chair, I raked my gaze over the sizeable glass-topped conference table. Manilla folders were spread over the surface, each one containing information on the vacant properties I was currently sitting on. I'd be damned if I allowed Riverside Grille to be added to the pile. I knew ordering takeout lunch for my staff wouldn't put much of a dent in their struggle, but hopefully, erasing their debt would. I didn't care if Byran was starting to get twitchy about the slow income Stone Enterprise was generating. That wasn't new. Whenever there was an interruption in cash flow, my accountant's blood pressure would skyrocket.

While it wasn't unusual for Bryan to overreact to such things, his worry was legitimate this time. With so many businesses either unable to pay their rent or closing altogether, Stone Enterprise had taken a big hit. I may own properties worldwide, but New York was home to most of my investments, and it was where I'd felt most of the negative impact. My predatory instincts were null and void now. There was no chasing a deal because there were no deals to be had—not unless I wanted to sell my soul to the devil. My investment in Wally's grocery stores seemed to be one of the only things thriving.

Who would have thought that my soft spot for the struggling grocer would one day be the thing that helped keep me afloat?

It was somewhat ironic when I thought about it. Wally's was the place where I'd met Krystina, the very woman who would eventually save me from myself. Now my investment in her ex-employer was doing all the saving.

Sort of.

While my portfolio still had plenty of properties that were performing just fine, I worried that it was only a matter of time before they started to struggle as well. Yes, the world had begun to right itself, but the road to full recovery was long. Still, I was fortunate to have invested wisely. It would be at least another year before I had to consider making any cuts to payroll. Hopefully, the markets and the economy will have turned in a positive direction before that happened.

Knowing I had the luxury to wait out the storm was a

privilege—especially when so many others were desperate, such as Hannah, the woman who stole the money from Stone's Hope. Based on what I knew about her, I didn't believe she was a common thief. It had been just over a week since Krystina first received the call from Claire about what happened, but Hannah was still missing, and her ex-boyfriend said he hadn't heard from her in months.

My gaze slid to the photograph of Krystina that sat on my desk, as it did so often on any given day. Glancing at the clock, I saw it was approaching noon. Picking up the phone, I dialed her for my regular daily check-in.

"Hey, handsome," she answered after the second ring. "How's your day going?"

"It's always miserable when you're not around, angel."

"Hmm... I miss the days when we both worked in the same building."

I frowned, easily able to read between the lines.

"How are you feeling?" I asked rather than take the bait.

"Fine, why?"

"I woke up around three in the morning and you weren't in bed. That's three nights in a row. Were you thinking about Hannah again or was it something else?"

For the past few nights, Krystina had left the comforts of our bed to go downstairs. The first two times, I'd found her sitting alone in the family room where she would apologize, saying she got up because she hadn't wanted to disturb me. Last night, I'd decided to let her be and instead lay awake worrying about all the things that could be troubling my wife. She'd always been a sound sleeper, and my concern over her stress level grew, especially after the terrible dream that I'd had to wake her from last week.

"I was thinking about Hannah, but more particularly, her daughter. I was there the day they came in. I met them both. Her daughter had these big, blue expressive eyes. Such a cutie. I can't help but worry about what will happen to her once Hannah is found."

"Are you sure that's all you were thinking about?" I pushed, needing to be sure it wasn't a nightmare that had pulled her from sleep. Nightmares could be triggered by many things, including stress and anxiety. Between the failed pregnancies, the effort of trying to conceive again, working remotely, and being home alone so much, I knew Krystina was carrying a lot of weight on her shoulders. What happened with Hannah at Stone's Hope only added to it.

"I'm sure. I'm convinced Hannah was acting out of pure desperation."

"I agree with you, angel, but we don't know that for sure. Her motivation is anyone's guess, and worrying about it is starting to take a toll on you. I wish you would just let Stephen sort it out and let the chips fall where they may."

"I know you're right, but I can't help it. I think it's bothering me so much because it's Christmastime.

Everyone deserves to be happy this time of year, and what she did negatively impacts so many people."

My throat thickened with a sudden surge of emotion. My fiercely independent and sassy wife could be tough as nails in the boardroom, but anyone privileged enough to get to know her would see her selflessness. She cared deeply about what happened at Stone's Hope, and it went beyond her personal experiences with abuse. Krystina cared because it was innately her.

"Have I told you lately how much I love your big heart?"

"No, not recently. Tell me again how wonderful I am," she teased.

I chuckled at her wit. Krystina never took a compliment well but instead made a sarcastic joke or flushed with embarrassment and changed the subject.

"So wonderful that I think you need to be pampered tonight," I said suggestively.

"Is that so?" Her voice had noticeably lowered, sounding somewhat breathy in anticipation. "I'm imagining a bubble bath. Drawn for two, I think. Candles. Music. Maybe a massage."

I suppressed a groan as the image of Krystina's lithe, naked legs wet and slippery with scented bubbles filled my mind. I spun in my chair, making a slow revolution before standing to look out the floor-to-ceiling windows at the Manhattan skyline. I used the view as a distraction from the restless energy that had suddenly come over me.

"Are you trying to torture me while I'm at work?" I asked.

"I would never!" she admonished. "But I must know. What are you wearing right now?"

"A suit. What else would I be wearing at the office?"

"What color suit?" she pushed.

I pressed my lips together, but was unable to stop the corners from twitching up. I could already predict where this was going and knew she was trying to distract me from what was really troubling her.

"Why do you ask, angel?"

"Because picturing you in a suit makes me all hot and bothered. Indulge me."

"It's a black Armani, fitted, with a red tie."

"I love that suit on you. Is the shirt fitted too?"

I chuckled. "Oh, no you don't. As much as I'd love to continue this conversation, I have to get some work done if you want me home at a decent time. Can we continue this later?"

"That's a promise, Mr. Stone."

Smiling, I ended the call and turned back toward my desk.

Despite Krystina's flirtations, I knew her heart was heavy. Stress over Hannah and not being able to give the kids at Stone's Hope a Christmas was slowly destroying her holiday spirit. Besides her waking up in the middle of the night, there had been other signs as well. Krystina almost always had Christmas music playing in the house and holiday-scented candles burning this time of the year. But, the past few days, it had been silent and without the familiar woody scents of mistletoe, berries, pine boughs, and holly when I got home from work. I needed to do something—anything—to brighten her dismal mood.

I'd considered donating money to the shelter so they could have their Christmas party as planned, but Stephen continued to adamantly advise against it for now. He'd rattled off some legal mumbo-jumbo about the IRS and how Stone Enterprise was connected to the Foundation. Until the issue with the missing money was sorted out, he thought it would be best not to donate anything. Because my hands were tied there, I would have to think of something else to cheer up Krystina.

I rubbed my palms over my face in frustration as I racked my brain. The problem was that my wife lacked for nothing—I made sure of it. I couldn't buy her happiness. This would require something more creative.

My laptop computer pinged, signaling the arrival of a new email. Moving over to the mouse, I clicked on the most recent email. It was from Hale.

TO: Alexander Stone
FROM: Hale Fulton
SUBJECT: Supply Order

Boss,

This month, I'll be placing a larger than normal order from our supplier in Queens. I need to replace several security lights around the house that were damaged in the windstorm we had a couple of weeks back. Helena's nursing staff also requested a few items to help with her occupational therapy, so I said I'd get what they needed while in the city. If you think of anything else I might need to grab when I'm there, let me know. I'll be making the supply run a week from today.

Hale

He didn't have to specify that the order would be placed online or that he would be getting it via curbside pickup. I never had to worry about him taking the proper health precautions to ensure Krystina and my mother's safety. He was a protector and fiercely loyal to us all. Knowing he was always careful and keeping watch over those I loved most gave me peace of mind. Plus, Vivian appreciated having him around because he could get to the cobwebs on the tall ceilings that she was too short to reach.

I pictured Hale's lengthy frame and absently wondered why Krystina hadn't called on him to help her assemble the ridiculously tall Christmas tree she'd purchased.

That's it!

Suddenly struck with an idea on how to cheer her up,

I rested my fingers on the computer's keyboard and began to type.

TO: Hale Fulton
FROM: Alexander Stone
SUBJECT: Re: Supply Order

Hale,

Thanks for keeping me apprised of the supply order. I will also be needing quite a few things, but it's nothing you'll need to go to the city for. However, I don't want you to wait until next Friday to get what I need. This weekend would be preferable. I'll get a list together and send it to you later today. You should be able to find most, if not all of it, locally.

Once you pick up everything I need, deliver it straight to the storage shed out back near the pond. Make sure Krystina doesn't see you. I'll explain why later. You should also plan on assisting me for a few hours on Monday and Tuesday afternoon. Possibly Wednesday, too. Get with Samuel, clear your schedules, and meet me at the shed at 2 P.M. on Monday. I'll give you more details when you get there.

Alexander Stone
CEO, Stone Enterprise

Sitting back, I smiled to myself, trying to decide how extravagant I wanted to get. Pulling up the local Christmas superstore website, I began to browse. Krystina often accused me of going over the top and spoiling her, and I had a feeling this time would be no different. After all, doting on my wife was one of my favorite pastimes.

Once I compiled the list of things I needed, I emailed it to Hale. Drumming my fingers on the desk, I tried to envision the way I wanted everything to play out next week, only to decide that there was no reason I had to wait to enact this plan I'd concocted. There were things I could easily do to implement Operation Cheer Up Krystina before next week.

Picking up the desk phone, I buzzed my assistant.

"Laura," I said when she answered.

"Yes, sir."

"I need you to set up a conference call between Vivian, Matteo, and me. Once you have them both on the line, let me know."

"Shall I tell them what this is regarding?"

Leaning back in my chair, a small smile spread across my face as I remembered the night that changed the course of my life.

"Just tell them it's about a menu—a menu from not so long ago."

8

Alexander

Five hours later, I pushed through the solid maple front door to my house to be enveloped in the mouth-watering aroma of garlic and sage. Just as I finished hanging my coat in the front hall closet, Vivian bustled across the foyer toward the dining room carrying a set of cream-colored table linens. She paused when she saw me come in.

"Good evening, sir," she greeted.

"Vivian," I replied with a nod. "How are things going? Is everything thing set for tonight?"

"I'm just putting the final touches on everything."

"Good, good. Where is Krystina now?"

"She's with your mother. She's been with Helena for oh..." She paused contemplatively. "I'd say about a half an hour now."

"Perfect," I said as I glanced down at my watch. "It's just after five now. I'll plan on bringing Krystina to the dining room at six. Will that give you enough time to finish your preparations?"

"Plenty of time, sir."

"Thank you. That will be all then," I dismissed, motioning for her to continue with what she was doing, and began to head to my mother's wing of the house.

My shoes echoed off the Italian marble floors as I passed the giant sixteen-foot-tall Christmas tree Krystina had erected in the foyer. I paused when my eye caught a glint from a small crystal heart placed directly on the center of the tree. I reached up to finger the cool glass and read the gold cursive font etched into the front.

Our First Christmas
2018

I remembered that Christmas as if it were only yesterday. We'd been six months into our marriage and had only lived in this house for a few weeks. Our holiday guests had just left, and we were sitting fireside in the living room, Krystina sipping on a glass of *Chateau Ste. Michelle* Riesling while I poured myself a nice tawny port. At some point during the night, the conversation had turned to children, and we'd decided we were ready to start a family. Krystina went off the pill a few days later and became pregnant within a month. It had been unexpected, as we both thought it would take a bit longer, but it was an exciting time, nonetheless.

But then she lost the baby a few weeks later and...

I squeezed my eyes shut tight, trying to block out the painful memories, but the effort was in vain. They always came rushing back, and this time was no different.

Krystina and I had made the conscious decision not to tell anyone that we were starting a family. We didn't want the pressure of people asking too many questions or offering unsolicited advice. When she lost the baby, it was as if the world had stopped spinning, and only we knew it. For me, it was almost a blessing that we hadn't told anyone, as it would mean admitting that I had failed.

It was hard to explain how I felt in the days and weeks following Krystina's miscarriages—especially after the third one. While I didn't experience the physical pain as she had, I had an unfamiliar emotional pain that I grappled with. I felt guilt over being excited or talking about things like baby names, thinking that my actions had only made Krystina's grief worse. I also felt anger over experiencing this in the first place, and thought I was a failure because I'd been unable to protect my wife and our baby.

And I fucking hated myself for it.

It made me feel weak and uncomfortable in my own

skin. The sinking feeling that came from knowing I'd let them down was an endless black pit.

My chest constricted and I shook my head, not wanting the stressful time to ruin my plans for the evening. Tonight, it was all about Krystina. Releasing the ornament to fall back against the branches, I stepped away from the tree and continued toward my mother's rooms.

When I came upon her suite, I lingered in the doorway to the main sitting area. Krystina sat in a chair directly in front of my mother's wheelchair. She was positioned away from me, allowing me only a glimpse of her side profile as she slowly flipped through the pages of a picture book that was on her lap.

A million emotions flooded through me as I watched her with my mother. Her expression was so expressive as she slowly turned each page, patiently waiting for my mother to react to one of the pictures. She looked so stunning sitting there, and it almost hurt to look at her. She was perfect, and at times, I wondered if she were really mine—as if this beautiful soul couldn't possibly have attached herself to someone like me. She was my very own slice of heaven on earth.

Krystina's cell phone began to ring, and she paused what she was doing with my mother to answer it.

"Hey, Ally," she answered.

I groaned inwardly.

Oh, no. This will never do.

Since it was Allyson on the phone, I knew Krystina could easily be tied up with her best friend for the next hour or more. Their phone chats were never short, and I had no intention of allowing Allyson to impede on my plans for the evening.

"I'm sitting here with Helena," Krystina continued. "We're looking at picture books. Isn't that right, Helena? I'm trying to find out if Alex has any lost Christmas traditions and was hoping the pictures might jog something in her memory."

Krystina fell quiet, and I assumed Allyson was talking on the other end of the line. I didn't want to allow them time to get into any sort of deep conversation, so I entered the room and snuck up behind Krystina. Squatting behind her, I snaked my arms around her waist. She jumped, and the picture book fell to the floor with a loud thud.

"Alex!" she screeched with a laugh.

"Hang up that phone. I have plans for us," I told her.

"But Ally literally just called me and—" She stopped short when I took the phone from her hand.

"Allyson, hi," I said into the phone.

"Right back at you, Alex. Are you having fun keeping my bestie locked up in that fancy cage?" she replied.

I smiled, knowing full well that Allyson agreed with my rules. She hadn't forgotten the front row seat she'd had to Krystina's first miscarriage, and she completely understood why my precautions were necessary. I was glad to have her in my corner about this, as it made convincing Krystina to follow my rules that much easier.

"Krystina and I always have fun. You know that. So, if you don't mind, I need to cut this conversation short. I have plans with my wife tonight."

"Oh, do tell! But wait—let me guess. Did Krys talk you into having another *Star Wars* marathon night?"

"Nope. Seeing those movies once was enough for me," I said with a chuckle.

"Oh, how dumb of me. I wasn't thinking about the time of year. It's a Christmas movie marathon for sure."

"Wrong again, Ally." I glanced down at Krystina and saw her curiously eyeing me, clearly wondering what my conversation with Allyson was all about.

"So what is it then?" Allyson prompted.

"I've planned a date night."

"Ooh, that definitely sounds fun! I'll leave you to it then. Later!"

"Goodbye, Allyson."

After hitting the end button on the phone, I handed it back to Krystina.

"We have a date tonight?" she asked.

"That's right. Vivian made something special. Come on, angel. Let's go change our clothes."

"Don't like my yoga pants and sweater?"

"I love you in anything you wear. I just have a particular thing that I want to see you dressed in tonight. Just trust me on this. You'll see. Besides, it will feel good to get dressed up for a change. Head on up to our room and pull out your red faux leather-trimmed skirt and a white cashmere sweater." I paused and furrowed my brow, trying to remember the rest of the outfit. "Strappy heels too. Black if I recall."

"Alex, what in the world—"

"This is not a debate," I stated firmly. "Go change—now. I'll meet you upstairs in a few minutes."

Standing at attention, she brought her hand up in a salute. "Yes, sir!"

There was no mistaking her sarcasm, and I nearly laughed as she left the room in a wildly exaggerated military march.

Shaking my head, I picked up the picture book and sat down in the chair that Krystina had vacated.

"My wife is something else, isn't she?" I asked, taking my mother's hand in mine.

She didn't respond, but I didn't expect her to. The only time Helena Russo was responsive to anything was when she wanted something, and even that was limited. Her child-like mind was driven only by things that gave her instant gratification.

A part of me was still so angry with her for allowing this to happen—for staying and giving my father the opportunity to break her. But a bigger part of me found it hard to stay mad. What little memories I had of her weren't all bad. I knew she loved Justine and me. And even though she was now only a shell of her former self, we loved her too.

Opening the book to where Krystina had left off, I pointed to pictures of stockings hung by a fireplace and frosted holiday cutout cookies. As I turned each page, I studied my mother's face and searched for a reaction of some kind. My childhood memories had painted her as a beautiful woman, and my recollections had served me well. Other than the horrific purplish-gray scar on the right side of her forehead—courtesy of my father—my mother was stunning. She had defined features with sharply angled cheekbones and a narrow nose. Justine and I looked so much like her, right down to her nearly black hair. Even though my mother's hair was streaked with gray, there was no denying that the three of us shared the same ebony coloring.

After turning pages for a few moments, I set the book to the side and hit the buzzer on my mother's wheelchair to call for her nurse. Within thirty seconds, Joanna Cleary, my mother's live-in aid, appeared. Her salt-and-pepper hair was pulled up into a tiny bun, and the crow's feet lines near her eyes deepened when she smiled at me.

"Mr. Stone. I hadn't realized you were here. I thought she was still spending time with the Missus."

"She was, but Krystina had to leave. I just called to let you know that I'll be leaving now too."

"Yes, sir," she replied and then turned to my mother.

"Come now, Miss Helena. Let's get you washed up. Dinner will be served soon."

Trusting that she was in good hands, I made my way up to the bedroom where Krystina was changing her clothes. Once there, I found my wife in her spacious walk-in closet. Just as I'd instructed, she was wearing the red skirt but had yet to adorn the sweater. She stood sifting through hangers in nothing but the skirt and her bra—and most importantly—the heels. My cock twitched at the sight of her. It didn't matter what kind of heeled shoes she wore. Every one of them screamed, 'fuck me now.'

My gaze traveled up the length of her legs and over the curve of her ass. Krystina thought she was a little too curvy, but I thought she was flawless. I loved every inch of her delectable body. If it were up to me, she'd be naked every minute of the day. Unfortunately, Krystina took issue with the suggestion that she walk around the house in the nude. My wife may submit to me in the bedroom and our playroom, but she was anything *but* submissive outside of that. She was a sassy warrior, never afraid to speak her mind, fiercely independent, wild, and strong—and so very beautiful.

And she's mine. All mine.

Stepping up behind her, I slid my hands over her hips, moving around to caress the smooth skin of her abdomen.

"Alex!" she startled as she quickly turned to face me. "I didn't hear you come in. You have to stop sneaking up on me like that!"

"Hmmm," I hummed as I leaned in and pressed my lips to the shell of her ear. "You look so good standing here in those heels. What do you say we skip the dinner portion of this date night and go right to dessert?"

I heard her breath catch. When she angled her head to give me access to her neck, I grinned. For as feisty as she could be, I loved that she submitted so easily under my touch. Moving my lips over the line of her jaw, I slid my tongue down the curve of her neck, nipping and suckling across her collar bone and shoulders.

Making my way back up to her ear, I whispered, "Do you remember that day, over four years ago, when I found you at La Biga and wanted to talk to you about a job offer?"

"I remember. I was mad at you for hijacking my phone," she breathed. Her hands were in my hair now, gripping at the roots and encouraging me to take more.

"I also told you that I wanted you naked," I reminded her as I rimmed the shell of her ear with my tongue.

"I remember that, too. You said, 'Any way I can have you. Preferably naked.' How could I forget? I thought you were crazy because we'd barely just met."

Stepping forward, I nudged her back until she was against the wall. Pressing the entire length of my body against hers, I shoved her skirt up until it bunched around her hips. Then, reaching between her legs, I cupped her sex. She instinctively pushed her pelvis against my hand, and I could feel her heat through her panties. Every thought I'd had that day coalesced into a solitary, forceful need, and I nearly dropped to my knees, wanting nothing more than to taste her. My cock thickened painfully, so desperate to be sheathed in her velvety warmth. It took all the restraint I could muster to hold back and stick to my plan.

"What happened after I said that?" I asked as I used my free hand to pinch one of her nipples through the lacy texture of her bra. To my satisfaction, it instantly tightened into a hard knot. I pulled the lace away from her breast and replaced it with my palm.

"You asked me out to dinner—no. That's not right. It was more like you ordered me to dinner," she added breathily as she lifted a leg to scissor it around my thigh. Thrusting her hips forward, she sought out the friction that the hand cupping her sex was unwilling to give. Her need was so damn hot, and it was killing me not to succumb to her desires.

All in good time, angel. All in good time.

"Your memory serves you right," I said, pushing her leg down and stepping away from her. She let out an audible gasp and I chuckled. "And what clothes were you wearing when we had dinner?"

Her brows pushed together as she pulled from her memories.

"Um, I think I was wearing a red skirt—" She stopped short and looked down. When she looked back up at me, I saw the realization in her eyes. "I was wearing the same clothes you asked me to put on tonight."

"Right again," I confirmed with a wide grin. "Now, finish getting dressed. I'll meet you downstairs in five minutes."

"What? You can't just get me all revved up like that and—"

"I can and I will. Now, be a good girl and do as you're told."

Not giving her a chance to respond, I left her to go into my closet and pick out what I would wear for the evening. If my memory was correct, I'd been wearing a poplin button-down and a pair of khakis that night at Matteo's restaurant.

After I changed clothes, I exited the closet to find Krystina standing fully clothed in front of the full-length mirror in our bedroom. She was smoothing her hands over her hips and pulling at the bottom hem.

"I'm reminded of why I never wear this skirt. I always thought it was too short," she said, yanking on the hem as if that would somehow make it longer.

"I know. That's why I wanted you to wear it," I said with a wink. "Are you ready to go downstairs?"

"Ready if you are."

Moving to her side, I extended my elbow for her to slip her arm through.

"Mrs. Stone, our date night awaits."

9

Krystina

Alexander and I walked down the grand staircase arm-in-arm. I was surprised to see Hale standing at the bottom of the steps. He looked distinguished and smart, dressed in his customary gray suit, but only those who knew him well would see the man beneath the well-dressed façade. A trained eye might suspect his military background, but his acute awareness and ruthlessness allowed him to hide it well. Besides his coming and going between the guest house and Helena's suite of rooms, Hale rarely came into the main house, but it was always a comfort to know he was nearby.

"Hale," Alexander said with a curt nod. "As we discussed, please escort Krystina to dinner."

"Yes, sir," Hale replied.

I eyed the two men in confusion. They shared a knowing look, and a ghost of a smile played on Alexander's lips.

"What are you two playing at?" I asked.

Alexander shook his head. "Trust me, angel, and go with Hale."

"This way, Miss Krystina," Hale said as he took hold of my arm.

I knew how Alexander and Hale operated together, and it appeared as if I didn't have a choice. When they decided to be tight-lipped about something, there was no chance in hell that I'd get either of them to budge. In the end, curiosity got the best of me. I didn't question things further and allowed Hale to guide the way.

We walked through the expansive family room and the open kitchen, past the large glass windows that gave a glimpse at the outdoor swimming pool before entering the back hallway that led to the garage.

"Are we going somewhere?" I asked, unable to keep the surprise out of my voice. I found it hard to believe that Alexander would have us actually go out somewhere to eat. There had to be something else going on. "Should I be getting a coat?"

Hale simply shook his head but didn't bother to hide the rare smile that curved the corners of his lips. I shivered from the cold garage as he led me to the Porsche SUV and opened the back door.

"Please get inside," he said with a sweep of his hand. "I started the car twenty minutes ago, so it should be plenty warm in there."

Oh, for Christ's sake. What the hell are they up to?

I puffed out an exasperated breath but continued to play along. When Hale simply drove around the front of the house, then stopped to let me out, I was genuinely confused. I walked beside him with a furrowed brow as he led me to the front door. Once inside, I was greeted by the grand staircase that Alexander and I had literally just come down.

"Follow me, Miss," Hale said.

I followed him until we reached the dining room. When we crossed the threshold, my eyes immediately went to Alexander, who stood just a few feet inside the doorway. He looked as perfect as usual. His dark waves framed his savagely gorgeous face and skimmed the collar of his gray button-down.

Stepping up to me, he placed his hand possessively on the small of my back. I loved when he touched me there. The steady pressure made me feel incredibly protected and cherished.

"I've got it from here, Hale. Thank you," Alexander said.

Looking around the spacious room, I immediately noticed that everything was different. A small candlelit table set for two was to the left of the long tigerwood dining table. It wasn't normally there. In fact, everything about the room was out of place. Our dining chairs were flipped up on end, and sheets covered portions of the other furniture. It was almost as if one were trying to give the appearance that a remodel was underway. It was strange. The room had been rearranged to look nothing like our dining room, yet it still had a familiar feel.

I glanced up at Alexander to see that he was watching me with those irresistible sapphire blues. He seemed to be gauging my reaction. I shifted my gaze back to the room, my eyes darting to each misplaced object.

What am I missing?

The lighting had been dimmed, and soft guitar music was playing from a speaker hidden somewhere in the room. I recognized the music as Tadeusz Machalski, one of Alexander's favorite musicians. He had discovered the guitar player in Venice, Italy, a fact I'd learned on our very first date at Matteo Donati's restaurant before he'd opened it up to the public.

And that's when it clicked.

The upside-down chairs, the table for two, my outfit, the music—Alexander was trying to recreate our first unofficial date. Even the aroma wafting from the kitchen was the same, and I wondered if Alexander asked Vivian to make some of Matteo's specialty dishes.

"Welcome to Krystina's Place," Alexander said, referring to the name of Matteo's restaurant that

Alexander had financially backed. "Well, it wasn't called that when we first went there, but you get the drift."

"Alex, this is amazing! Everything looks just like it did on our first date."

"The only thing missing is one exuberant Italian waiter, but Vivian promised to do her best to replace him," Alexander said with a wink.

"Oh, no!" I giggled. "Poor Vivian. I really hope you aren't going to make her play the role of Matteo."

"Don't worry. I'll be the only one calling you *bella* tonight."

I shook my head, still surprised by the attention to recreate the details of that night.

"What in the world prompted you to do all of this in the first place?"

"You've just seemed down lately—definitely not yourself—and I wanted to do something different to cheer you up. Come have a seat, angel."

Taking hold of my elbow, Alexander guided me toward the small table and pulled out a chair for me to sit. As he pushed me in closer to the table, I had a sense of déjà vu, and I couldn't help but recall how nervous I'd been to dine with Alexander that night so many years ago.

Nervous is an understatement. I'd been an absolute jittery wreck.

The corners of my mouth turned up from the memory.

"What are you smiling about?" Alexander asked as he took his seat across from me.

"I was thinking about how nervous I was in the hours leading up to that first date and then how it seemed to worsen in the days that followed. You were so intimidating, and it scared the hell out of me. Now that I know how everything played out, it was kind of silly for me to be so anxious. I have to wonder what would have happened if I wasn't nervous but had given in to your temptations instead."

A whisper of a smile played at his lips as he pulled a bottle of cabernet sauvignon from the ice bucket on the table and poured us each a glass.

"My temptations?" he questioned.

"Yeah. You were like the devil—always taunting me. What if I had gone home with you that night? Would you have pursued me as you did if we'd had sex right out of the gate?"

"First of all, I wouldn't have brought you home that night. I certainly wanted to, but at that point, nobody came home with me until there was some level of trust built up. My lifestyle put me too much at risk, as I explained back then." He paused and took a sip of wine. I did the same, savoring the bold flavor on my tongue as I waited for him to continue. "Secondly, I would have pursued you no matter what. You were like a drug to me. The minute I saw you, I had to have you no matter what the consequences were. And third, if I had decided I wanted to fuck you that night, I would have."

His blunt words were as crude as they were alluring— and it was so damn hot. I loved it when he talked to me like that. The ache he'd created between my legs when we were upstairs in my closet had yet to go away, and his salacious remarks only seemed to intensify it.

Before I could respond, Vivian came into the room carrying a platter and two small plates.

"Here you go," she announced. *"Insalata caprese and antipasto italiano."*

I smiled at yet another thing that mirrored my night with Alexander four years ago.

"Thank you, Vivian," I said. "I'm sure it will be just as good as Matteo's."

"Don't thank me yet. Adding some cold cuts and cheese to a plate was the easy part. It took Alexander an hour to convince Matteo to give up his secret recipe for eggplant *parmigiana.* After all that trouble, I can only hope I did it justice."

"I'm sure it will be fine, Vivian. Thank you," Alexander told her.

After Vivian retreated to the kitchen, Alexander and I dove into the appetizers. We didn't talk much but simply enjoyed each other's company while eating. Occasionally, I could feel Alexander's eyes, and I knew I was the focus of his dark, penetrating gaze without even looking. When I did look up, the flavorful mozzarella that I'd just popped into my mouth may as well have been cardboard. My breath hitched, and my heart began to race—a reaction Alexander could elicit with just one smoldering look. It was as if he were imagining himself undressing me, removing each article of clothing with careful precision. Then there were the little things—the lingering of his hand touching mine as he passed me the balsamic vinegar or the not-so-accidental brush of his foot against my leg under the table. All of it was designed to torture.

By the time the eggplant arrived, I had no interest in eating anything. All I wanted to do was lunge across the table, hike up my skirt, and ride him like there would be no tomorrow. However, the minute I speared a piece of the hot breaded vegetable and put it into my mouth, my stomach pitched. No matter how hard I tried, I could not bring myself to swallow the food. Just the mere idea of forcing it down made me want to vomit all over the table.

Shit. Add eggplant to the list of pregnancy food aversions.

Taking my napkin from my lap, I spit out the food as discreetly as I possibly could. This used to be one of my favorite dishes, and questions would surely be raised if I suddenly didn't want to eat it.

Not for the first time this week, I contemplated telling Alexander about the baby right then and there, but thought better of it when I recalled the video conference call that I'd had with my OBGYN just the day before. She had reminded me that a healthy first trimester was crucial to development. Even though I may not be showing much on the outside, the baby's major organs and systems were forming, and this was when the fetus was most vulnerable. At eleven weeks, I still had a week or two to go before the risks to the baby decreased significantly. Until then, it would be selfish of me to get Alexander's hopes up. I had to protect him as much as I could.

So, instead of eating the eggplant, I focused on the penne pasta side dish. Thankfully, I could stomach that without a problem, but I knew it was only a matter of time before Alexander noticed I wasn't eating the main dish.

I'll need to hide the evidence.

Hide the evidence? What are you, a five-year-old?

Ugh.

Glancing at him through lowered lashes, I casually cut the eggplant into small pieces. Then, like a child who hid uneaten brussels sprouts from their mother, I tucked it between the folds of my napkin when Alexander wasn't looking. It was ridiculous, as Vivian was sure to see it when she cleared the table. I tried to think of someplace to stash the eggplant, so she didn't find it either, but I was coming up short of ideas. Stuffing an eggplant-filled napkin under my skirt or sweater was out of the question, as both were too fitted.

When Alexander's fork began to scrape the bottom of the plate, I knew I was running out of time. Standing up abruptly, I began to clear our dishes, balancing my plate on top of the eggplant-filled napkin.

"I'm stuffed," I announced, making sure to slow my

words before continuing. I was a terrible liar, and one of my tells was to fidget or talk too fast. "I'm just going to bring my plate back to the kitchen. If you're through, I can bring yours too."

"Don't be ridiculous. Vivian will clear the table," he admonished.

"I've got it. I'm sure she has plenty to clean up in the kitchen."

I took his empty plate and stacked it on mine, careful to keep the stuffed napkin under the plate stack. Then, without another word, I hurried from the table and away from Alexander's surprised and questioning gaze.

Exiting the dining room, I hurriedly made my way down the long hallway leading to the kitchen. I was in such a rush to dispose of the uneaten food that I wasn't paying attention. When I rounded the corner to the galley, I collided forcefully with Vivian.

"Oh!" we both said in unison.

The plates smashed up against my chest, the remains of pasta sauce soaking into my white cashmere sweater. We both stumbled back, and in my tall heels, I struggled to keep my footing. Before I could stop myself, I slipped and went down hard.

The plates fell from my hands and onto the marble floors. The sound of them shattering into hundreds of pieces echoed down the hall.

"Oh, dear!" Vivian exclaimed, bracing herself on the

edge of the wall to stop herself from joining me on the floor. "Are you alright?"

I glanced around me to see little bite-sized chunks of eggplant and other food bits littering the floor with the broken china.

"I'm okay," I said, shifting to my right and rubbing a hand over my backside. There was no doubt that my ass would be black and blue before morning.

As I moved to stand up, I noticed Vivian frowning at the mess on the floor.

"I guess Matteo's eggplant is better," she said lightly with a small smile.

"No, no! Yours was great!" I said too quickly.

Oh, good God. I'm so terrible at this!

Thankfully, Alexander came rushing down the hall. His presence dominated anything else that may have been happening as he hovered over me with a concerned expression.

"Angel, are you okay? What happened?"

"I wasn't paying attention and bumped into Vivian. I'm fine, really," I tried to assure him.

Leaning down, Alexander positioned his hands under my arms and pulled me to my feet. Worry lines marred his handsome face as he scrutinized me. He ran his hands up and down my arms, up to my head, and pushed my hair aside as if he were inspecting for damage.

"Are you sure?" he asked.

I pulled my head away, embarrassed by his doting in

front of Vivian. Turning to her, I said, "I'm so sorry, Vivian. I should have been more careful."

"Don't you worry your pretty little head about it," she assured me as she moved to get a broom from the pantry. "The two of you go back to your romantic dinner while I get this cleaned up."

"I can help—" I started.

"Nonsense! Now, out with you both," Vivian shooed, motioning with the broom.

"Leave her to it, angel," Alexander assured as he tugged at my arm. Tossing me a quick wink, he added more quietly so only I could hear, "The night is still young, and I have plans for you tonight."

I looked between him and Vivian, torn between the devilish gleam in my husband's eyes and helping our aging housekeeper clean up the result of my clumsiness. Ultimately, he won out—as if there'd actually be another scenario.

Alexander looped his arm around my waist and led us back into the dining room. But rather than resume my seat, I paused and looked up at him.

"I don't want to ruin whatever else you may have planned, but I'd like to change out of this sweater if that's okay with you."

Alexander looked down at my sauce-stained sweater as if noticing it for the first time.

"Of course," he said with a brief nod before leading me past the table and out the door. When we reached the bottom of the grand staircase, I glanced up.

"I hope I didn't ruin dessert," I joked.

"There will be plenty of dessert, angel. You can count on that. I'll just need to adjust my plan a bit—not that I mind. I kind of like the way my new plan is taking shape."

"Oh?"

"You mentioned something about a bubble bath when we were on the phone earlier."

"I did," I said with a smile, remembering our flirtations from the afternoon.

"Seeing as I've had to modify this evening's agenda, I'll need a few minutes. Go strip out of those clothes, then meet me in the master bath."

Ten minutes later, I had scrubbed my stained sweater and left it soaking in the laundry room. Wrapped in an ivory satin robe, I returned to our master suite. My bare feet quietly padded across the bedroom carpet as I made my way to the bathroom.

I slowly pushed open the door and saw Alexander sitting on the edge of our large soaking tub, pouring jasmine-scented bubble bath into the steaming stream of water. A towel was draped around his waist, leaving his chest bare. I took a moment to admire the chiseled lines of his pectorals and abdomen. Even after four years, I'd yet to tire of looking at him. His Adonis-like torso could make any sculptor weep.

Stepping inside the bathroom, I closed the door

behind me. Moving past the twin pedestal sinks, I made my way to him. As I walked, I noticed a dish of chocolate-covered strawberries sitting on the tiled ledge surrounding the tub. When I reached Alexander, he plucked one of the strawberries from the plate and stood.

Moving so we were toe-to-toe, I took in the predatory look in his eyes. He was so close, and his nearness sent my heart racing. Blood thrummed loudly in my ears. I could feel the heat radiating from his body, his delicious scent mixed with the jasmine bath tantalizing my nose and taking over my senses. It was making my head spin. His warm breath mingled with mine as he leaned in and pressed a chocolate-covered strawberry to my lips.

"Open," he said.

I obeyed his command and parted my lips. He urged it just past my teeth, and I took a bite as his free hand untied the belt at my waist. Parting my robe, he pushed it from my shoulders until it pooled onto the floor. Standing completely naked before him, we simply stared at each other for a long moment as I slowly chewed. When I swallowed, he leaned in closer until his mouth was only a whisper away.

Drawing in a deep breath, he snaked an arm around my waist and drew me in. Then, lifting me until I was balancing on my tiptoes, he slanted his mouth over mine and took what belonged to him. His lips were tender at first, soft and delicious until he deepened the kiss and demanded more. Our tongues danced and twisted until I thought I might drown in everything that was Alexander.

His hands moved over my body, every caress telling a story—that I was beautiful, cherished, and sexy. His touches spun such a tale of love and devotion that he could make poets weep. I was desperate to feel him—on me, inside me—until I was lost in the sensation of falling over that blissful edge. Soft, pleading sounds poured from my throat.

"I want to be inside you, Krystina. It's all I've wanted all night." The rough timbre of his voice made goosebumps pebble on my skin.

"So, what's stopping you?"

His sharp intake of breath let me know that he was hanging on by a thread. What little shred of control he had left was only a façade, and he left me no time to react. His hand threaded through my hair, roughly pulling my head back. Within seconds, his mouth crushed against mine once again. He kissed me with such passion that heat exploded through my veins. I surrendered to him, returning his kiss with a fervent hunger. There was just something about this moment—this night—that reminded me of all the reasons I fell in love with this man. He was my husband and the father of my child. It didn't matter if he didn't know about the baby yet—I knew it, and knowing I was growing a part of him inside of me amplified my love in the most inexplicable ways. All that existed was him.

I moaned into his mouth, tasting him with flicks of my tongue as a heaviness began to build in my chest and well in my throat until I thought I might burst. And as the two of us slid into the tub, the water around us lapped, and the rest of the world disappeared.

10

Krystina

A week later, Vivian and I sat at the table in the breakfast nook with a fat three-ring cookbook filled with mine and Alexander's favorite recipes. It was meal planning day, a Thursday routine we'd established over a year ago when daily trips to the grocer had failed Alexander's so-called 'risk assessment.' While I still thought these controlled outings were unnecessary, I'd learned when not to challenge my husband. This was one of those times—especially now that I had better insight into what was driving Alexander's fears.

In the end, Vivian didn't seem to mind Alexander's rules, and I liked being a part of the grocery selection process. Being involved made my kitchen feel less like a restaurant, which is how it had felt for the first two years after I'd married Alexander. Plus, I enjoyed spending time with Vivian. She understood Alexander in ways most people didn't, and I'd often used her as a sounding board when he was having one of his over-the-top moments. The aging housekeeper was as sweet as she was feisty—but absolutely terrible with technology. She still utilized a spiral notebook to create handwritten grocery lists, which I would then take and input into the grocery store's online ordering app.

"We should get the ingredients for the parmesan risotto with spinach and tomatoes. Alex and I both liked that," I told Vivian.

"Oh, that recipe was a great find!" Vivian said with a clap of her hands, then quickly picked up her pen to write down what she would need. "I haven't made that in a while. I have most of the ingredients too. I'll just need to pick up the produce for it. Now, what about Christmas Eve and Christmas Day dinner? Any thoughts about that?"

I felt my shoulders involuntarily sag at the thought of what Christmas would be like this year. Two years ago, we'd had a houseful. My mother, Frank, and Justine had come over. Our friends, Allyson and Matteo, Bryan, Stephen, and their perspective dates, had also joined us. All were invited to a Christmas feast prepared by Vivian that most top chefs would envy. Together with Vivian, Hale, and Helena, the fourteen of us sat around the dining room table indulging in a delicious surf and turf meal suitable for royalty. After dinner, a few of my ex-coworkers from Wally's had joined us for cocktails, and we stayed up late sharing laughs and good company. It was how Christmas was meant to be.

But last year, it had only been Alexander and me because of the pandemic. We both agreed that having a large gathering wasn't wise and had opted to take a trip to Vermont instead. Since flying was out of the question, we took our time driving from New York to Stowe. We enjoyed the scenic views of the snow-covered mountains and small villages until reaching the cozy one-bedroom chalet Alexander had rented for us for the week. It had been an incredibly romantic getaway, but without my family and loved ones around, it didn't feel like Christmas to me. After that, I vowed to never spend a Christmas without them again—yet here we were.

If it weren't for Alexander's rules...

I understood why he had them, but I didn't at the same time. It was stifling. If I weren't pregnant, I'd be fighting him tooth and nail over this. The baby was the only reason I continued to abide by his rules.

While Alexander's controlling instincts were often the source of arguments between us, I'd learned how to rein him in. I may grant him total control in the bedroom, but it ended there. I was, and always would be, my own person. The problem was that the holidays made my isolation seem that much more pronounced.

Still, perhaps Alexander would loosen up and make an exception for Christmas Day if we took precautions. We didn't have to have a lot of people over. Maybe just Allyson and Matteo. The two of them seemed to have become a package deal over the past few years, even though they both denied that there was anything romantic between them. It was doubtful that Alexander would agree to even a small get-together, but I could try. After all, it was Christmas.

"Let me think about it, Vivian," I eventually said. "I'm not sure what Alex wants to do. So don't order anything yet, even if it means having to place a second order next week."

Vivian nodded. She knew Alexander almost better than anyone and could understand my predicament.

"Yes, Miss. I'll wait for you to let me know."

"As soon as I talk to him, I'll get with you. Other than Christmas, I think we've got all the meals for next week covered. You'll just need to get with Helena's nurse and therapist about anything they might need."

"They should be all set. I already have their food requests, and Hale took a supply list from them. He'll be gone most of the day tomorrow picking up what they need from various places."

"Well, good. That makes it easier for you. Once you finalize the list, I'll place the online order for you. What time do you want the pickup scheduled for tomorrow?"

"Let's do one o'clock."

"Perfect."

Glancing at the wall clock hanging above the table, I saw it was going on three. I had a few things to add to the Beaumont Jewelers campaign. Sheldon Tremaine, the owner, decided at the last minute that he wanted to increase his budget and do a big push the final three days before Christmas. If I got back to my office now, I just might have enough time to put it together before the end of the day.

Standing from my seat at the table, I was about to excuse myself when my cellphone began to ring. Removing it from my pocket, I saw it was Stone's Hope. A shiver of worry raced across my skin as I slid my finger across the screen to answer it.

"Hello?"

"Hi, Krystina. It's Claire. I'm so sorry to bother you."

"It's okay, Claire. What's up?"

"I have an update on Hannah."

"Okay, shoot."

"The police are still considering this an ongoing investigation, but they have enough information to issue a warrant for her arrest. I just can't believe it took them two weeks to move on it. She's clearly guilty, and I'm happy they're finally doing something."

"Hmmm," was my only reply.

I couldn't say that I shared Claire's sentiment. It didn't make me happy to know a struggling single mother was facing jail time right before the holidays. Just thinking about it caused a tightening in my heart.

Then, without warning, I felt my eyes tear up as I was reminded once again about how her poor child may end up motherless at Christmas. I sniffled and the tears continued to well. I hurriedly wiped the moisture away before Vivian could see.

Damn hormones.

Lately, it seemed like everything made me cry. Even things as simple as dropping something on the floor had me all choked up. And forget Hallmark movies—what a huge mistake that was. Their happily-ever-after tear-jerkers did more than make me tear up. It had taken me hours to calm down after watching the last one, and I'd sworn off their evil writers for good after that day.

Seriously. Didn't they know pregnant women might be watching?

"Mrs. Stone, are you okay?" Claire asked, snapping me to attention.

"Yes, I'm fine," I told her, fighting to keep my voice even. "We'll just have to wait and see what happens with the investigation. Have you contacted Stephen to let him know about the warrant?"

"No need. The police are in direct contact with him. He had an investigator here asking questions a couple of times last week, too. He went through our computers and interviewed the rest of the staff and me."

"Good. Stephen is reliable and competent. I expect

that whoever he sent was thorough. The staff cooperated okay?"

"Yes, of course. And well, speaking of the staff," Claire said hesitantly. "I didn't only call to give you an update on Hannah. I have a problem, and I was hoping you could help."

"Sure. What's going on?"

Claire sighed. "When the staff found out that we were going to cancel Christmas for the women and kids at the shelter, they became very distraught."

"That's understandable. I'm upset by it, too," I told her sincerely. "It's not like I want to cancel, but until the investigation is complete, we had to make a choice. It was either keep the heat on or buy Christmas presents."

"No... it's more than just that," she said tentatively.

"Go on. What else is there?"

"They are threatening to quit over it. They know how wealthy Mr. Stone is, and well, they think he should be able to personally fund it, saying it would be a drop in the bucket from someone like him."

I blinked, taking a moment to absorb her words.

"I see," was all I said, putting forth considerable effort to keep the iciness out of my voice.

I knew it wasn't Claire's fault that the staff had these perceptions. Alexander *could* afford to fund just about anything. That was public knowledge. The staff just didn't understand the legalities surrounding it. However, when I considered how charitable and giving my husband had been over the years to numerous charities around the city, Claire and the staff had no right to judge him. Alexander may have captivated me from day one, but he was more than just a rich sexy suit. I knew the man inside in ways that others didn't, and I had fallen in love with his sharp intelligence, ruthlessness, and profoundly generous side.

Still, I knew I should cut them some slack. There was no way for Claire or the staff to know the real Alexander. He guarded his privacy so tightly that everyone who clamored to know the real him ended up learning next to nothing.

"I'm sorry, Krystina. Really, I am," Claire continued. "But with the shelter already short-staffed, I can't afford to lose a single person. They're stressed, and I think this sent them over the edge. After almost two years of dealing with pandemic restrictions, people are tired. Nobody has patience for much of anything anymore. Do you know how hard it is to manage all the rules in a congregate setting? Seriously, why are we still being told to social distance? It's dumb."

I listened to Claire vent her frustrations, even though the restrictions had nothing to do with me. I didn't write the rules and had no control over them. The problem was that many of them went against human nature. Although I hadn't been to the shelter in quite some time, I imagined the limitations must feel amplified in a setting where women needed help above all else, yet comforting someone with a simple hug was forbidden. I used to be a regular guest speaker there but had been restricted to video conference appearances only. In a way, even I had abandoned them by hiding behind a cold, impersonal screen.

"I understand, Claire. But about the issue with the staff," I reminded, needing her to get back to the reason she had called me in the first place. "If there were anything we could do to change things, we would. Unfortunately, due to the legalities and rules surrounding a non-profit, Alexander's attorney has advised him against supplementing or donating any money right now. He has to wait until the investigation is complete."

"Wednesday, Krystina," she blurted out. "The Christmas party was supposed to be on Wednesday. The staff said that would be their last day if the party at the shelter isn't back on. I believe them, too. After all, why stay when they can go pretty much anywhere else and make more money."

I pinched the bridge of my nose and inhaled deeply. Claire was right to worry about the employees quitting. I knew the pay was only average at the shelter. Even if we paid more, there was no way we could replace the entire staff—not now when employers across the country were struggling to find help. I needed to do damage control, which would most likely mean going to the shelter myself. Perhaps if I talked to the employees personally and explained things, they would understand.

Of course, Alexander would be furious if I ventured

out of the house now. In fact, furious may even be too mild of a word. If he were to find out I was pregnant and had left, he would not only lock me up in this gilded cage for the remainder of the pregnancy—he'd throw away the key. I knew this to be true, and I half wondered if I'd subconsciously made a choice to wait on telling him about the baby because of that. Perhaps keeping my secret was my way of trying to hang onto the little shred of independence I had left. I wasn't sure. All I knew was that I had to figure out a way to leave the house without him knowing. Stone's Hope needed me.

"Give me a few days to think on this," I finally said to Claire. "I'll have an answer for you by Monday."

"Thanks, Krystina. I appreciate it."

When I ended the call, I turned back to Vivian to see a concerned expression on her face. I'd nearly forgotten she was there.

"Is everything okay?" she asked.

"Not really. We're having an issue over at Stone's Hope. I need to figure out how to fix it. If you'll excuse me, Vivian. I need to get to my office and make a few calls."

Vivian gave me a short nod, but there was no denying the worry lines on her face as I turned to make my way toward my home office. Once there, I sat behind the desk and moved the mouse to wake the computer.

I'd had an idea while I was on the phone explaining to Claire why Alexander couldn't donate the money. Stephen had said Alexander couldn't donate because both he and

Stone Enterprise were too closely tied to the Stoneworks Foundation. He feared any money transfers would trigger a full-scale IRS audit, a headache neither he nor the accounting team wanted to deal with. However, he didn't say anything about Turning Stone Advertising donating money. That company was solely in my name now, and it had nothing to do with Alexander or his businesses whatsoever.

Just as I was about to pull up my contact list for Stephen's phone number, an email from Alexander caught my attention. Clicking on it, I quickly skimmed his message.

TO: Krystina Stone
FROM: Alexander Stone
SUBJECT: Later

My Beautiful Angel,
Plan on calling it quits early. I'll be home in about an hour. You've been caged up in the house for too long, and I have a surprise for you. Dress warmly. A winter wonderland awaits.

Until later,
Alexander Stone
CEO, Stone Enterprise

Dress warmly? A winter wonderland?

I sat back in my chair, feeling perplexed over whatever Alexander was scheming. I looked at the time stamp of the email. He'd sent it thirty minutes ago. If he would be home that soon, that only gave me a half of an hour to work and wouldn't give me enough time to finish what I needed to do for Beaumont Jewelers—especially when I had calls to make about Stone's Hope. The ad campaign would have to wait until morning. The shelter was my number one priority right now. With any luck, I would have the approval to make a monetary donation to Stone's Hope before the end of the day today.

My only problem would be figuring out a way to go to the shelter in person to announce it. I wanted to appeal to the staff personally to ensure they weren't going to go anywhere now that Christmas was back on. However, pulling off a quick escape from the house would be difficult. I absently tapped my finger on the desk as I considered my options.

Perhaps tomorrow when Vivian is picking up the groceries. Hale will be gone on a supply run as well, and...

I let my thought go unfinished and sighed. I was bound to get caught. I knew it, but Alexander would just have to deal with it. The staff and the struggling women at Stone's Hope needed and morale boost, and the risk was worth whatever punishment my husband would indeed have in store for me.

11

Alexander

I arrived home just a few minutes after four o'clock and found Krystina rummaging in the closet off the foyer. Her back was to me, and she was bent over, appearing to be looking through a small storage bin. I took in the sight of her tight, blue jean-covered ass. Unable to help myself, I walked up to her and slid my hands over the curves of her behind. She gasped when I squeezed, then caught her hips and pressed into her.

"That better be my husband standing behind me," she said with a giggle.

"And if it's not?"

"Hmmm... those hands feel way too good. If it's not my

husband, then I may have to trade him in for this stranger with the magic touch," she toyed as she pushed against me, giving her ass a little wiggle. My cock twitched from the tease, and I nearly groaned. My wife was so goddamn sexy, and she didn't even know it.

"Is that so?" I whispered. Sliding both hands under the hem of her shirt, I grazed over her ribs and cupped each breast. Her nipples tightened beneath the fabric of her bra, and I felt her shiver beneath me. "Tell me. Are these the hands of a stranger?"

"I'm not sure," she said breathily, promoting this titillating little game further. "My husband wouldn't stop there. If he really wanted me, he'd give my ass a good smack, then order me to the playroom."

My length hardened at her words, even if I had no intention of granting her subtle request. The customized playroom would be off-limits for the foreseeable future, but that didn't stop me from envisioning her tied up and breathless after experiencing the sting of my flogger.

Stepping back, I chuckled with amusement and turned her to face me. "It seems as though my angel is a little sexed up today."

"Maybe just a little," she said with a small smile as she ran her fingers down the length of my tie.

"As much as I'd like to spank that perfect little ass of yours until it's a nice rosy shade of red, we'll have to save that for later. Like I said in my email—I have a surprise for you. I'm just going to change out of this suit, and then I'll meet you back here. Be dressed warmly and ready to head out in five minutes."

Krystina eyed me curiously, and I knew a million questions were swirling in her head.

All in good time, angel. All in good time.

As promised, I had changed into jeans and a Brunello Cucinelli quarter-zip and was back in the foyer a few minutes later. Krystina stood waiting for me, wearing a white wool hat and the Canada Goose parka that I'd bought for her last year before our trip to Vermont.

"Where are your gloves?" I asked her.

"I'll just put my hands in my pockets. I'll be fine."

I pursed my lips in annoyance.

"When I said dress warmly, I meant it. I don't want you to catch a chill." I ignored her petulant eye roll and crossed the foyer to the same bin I'd found Krystina rummaging through when I first came home. It only took me a minute to find a pair of gloves that matched her hat. I handed them to her. "Put these on."

"Yes, sir!" she said mockingly, then took the gloves from me.

I raised an eyebrow at her. "You're asking to be punished. You know that, right?"

"Please," she said with a playful wink, and I had to smile.

Satisfied Krystina would be warm enough, I grabbed my own coat and gloves and we headed out. The air was crisp in the low-hanging sun, the last few warm rays slowly disappearing to make room for the night. I took Krystina's gloved hand in mine, and we walked around to the back of the house. When I continued past the garage, she angled her head curiously.

"I assumed we would be driving somewhere. Where are we going?"

"You'll see," was all I said.

We followed the shoveled path that extended from the house to the large pond near the back of the property. I'd made sure to instruct the grounds maintenance crew always to keep the path clear for my mother. She enjoyed small outings, and when the weather permitted it, her nurse would take her out in her wheelchair and push her around the pond.

I'd noticed that the long walks had become more frequent as of late, and it reminded me of what Krystina had said regarding my mother's staff not being allowed to leave the house. Now I wondered if the walks they took my mother on were really for her or if it was their attempt at getting out. A pang of guilt hit me, knowing my demands were slightly unreasonable, but it didn't matter as long as there were still dangerous risks to those I loved.

I looked up at the tall pines that lined the path. Endless branches seemed to go on forever, their needles piercing the sky and blocking any wind by creating a shielding wall. We were a reasonable distance from the house, but I could still smell the smoke from the chimneys. It mixed with a burst of pine from the surrounding trees, creating the perfect winter scent. The only sound that could be heard in the protective cocoon was the crunch of our boots in the tracks of snow left behind by the snow removal crew.

Everything was peaceful, and I could easily see why both my mother and Krystina loved coming here so much. So far away from the hustle and bustle of the city, it was the ultimate time out. I found the tranquility of the space to be similar to what I'd felt when I took *The Lucy*, my yacht, out to the New York Bight during the summer months.

Just before we reached the pond, the sun had set entirely, giving way to a dark, moonless night. I stopped walking and stepped in front of Krystina. Then, reaching into my pocket, I pulled out the red necktie I'd been wearing earlier that day.

"Close your eyes, angel."

Krystina's curious expression was back, but she did as I asked without question. Moving closer to her, I placed the tie over her eyes. Positioning it so she couldn't peek, I wrapped it around to the back of her head and secured the ends in a knot. Looping my arm through hers to guide her, we continued on until the trees opened up to reveal the big open space surrounding the pond. Losing the protective cover of the trees, the temperature seemed to drop in the light wind that swirled around us.

"Stay here," I told her, then placed a kiss on her forehead. "I'll be right back."

I stepped away and began the short walk around the pond to the storage shed where the extension cords were waiting to be plugged in. I glanced at the water's surface as I walked. When I was here yesterday preparing for today, the pond had been covered in a thin layer of ice. Today's sun had melted it, but the crispness in the air signaled that it wouldn't be long before it completely froze over for the year.

When I reached the shed, I smiled with anxious anticipation. Opening the doors, I was greeted by blackness and had to flip on the light switch so I could see. In the far corner, the ends of several extension cords awaited me. I couldn't wait to show Krystina the winter wonderland that I'd created for her. I could have paid a crew to do it, but I wanted this to have my personal touch, knowing she would appreciate it more that way. With Hale's help, we had brought all the tools needed to string lights around the pine trees, all while Krystina worked in the house, completely unaware of my secret project. Oversized light-up presents and large blowup ornaments that rivaled the size of those on 6th Avenue lined the path that wrapped around the pond. When it was all lit up, the scene looked like a postcard.

After plugging the extension cords into the outlet, I walked back out into the night. However, everything remained dark. Not a single strand of lights had turned on.

What the hell?

Hale had assured me that he'd tested everything last night. Going back inside the shed, I wiggled the cords around to see if there happened to be a loose connection, but my effort was in vain. The night was still black, and I had no idea what I needed to do to get the lights to turn on.

"Dammit," I muttered.

I was a man of many talents, but electrical work was not one of them. Pulling my cell from my pocket, I dialed Hale's number. Hopefully, he would be able to fix this.

"What's up, boss?" he answered after the second ring.

"Hale, I'm in the storage shed. All I have to do is plug in the extension cords, right?"

"That's right."

"It isn't working."

"What do you mean?"

"I mean, when I plug them in, nothing happens," I said impatiently.

"That's strange. It could be one of two things. It's possible that we tripped a breaker. If that's the case, it's an easy fix. I'll run over to the main house and check the main panel in the basement now."

"And if it's not that?"

"It means it's a problem with the lights. When one bulb goes out, they all go out. So we'd have to either restring all the lights or test each bulb to locate the defect. Let's just hope it's only a tripped breaker."

"Shit," cursed under my breathe. There had to be at

least twenty thousand bulbs out here. "Alright. Check the breaker box and let me know what you find."

"I'm walking over to your house now."

Ending the call, I made my way back to Krystina. When she heard me approaching, she angled her body toward me.

"Alex? What's going on?"

"A little problem, angel. Just hang on."

She nodded, but I noticed a slight chatter to her teeth. I thought about the thin shirt she'd been wearing, and considered the cold bite brought on by the slight breeze. While the down-hooded coat provided ample protection from the cold, she still should have worn a heavier shirt. Looking down at her feet, I noticed she wore fashion boots. The stylish footwear clearly wasn't meant for warmth.

Damn it.

I mentally cursed myself for not noticing her shoe choice before leaving the house. Pulling her close, I rubbed my hands up and down her arms to try and ward off her chill.

A few minutes later, my phone buzzed with an incoming text.

TODAY
5:05 PM, HALE:

It's not the breaker. Must be a problem with the lights. What do you want me to do?

Fuck!

I glanced at Krystina, who was still blindfolded and waiting, then looked back down at my phone.

5:06 PM, ME:

> Nothing for now. Krystina's surprise will have to wait. We can work on how to fix this over the weekend.

5:07 PM, HALE:

> Okay, boss. Sorry your night got messed up.

Pocketing my phone, I shook my head.

Me too, Hale. Me too.

"Change of plans, angel," I said, turning her body toward the path back to the house. I looped my elbow through hers and tried to keep the annoyance out of my voice. "We're going to have to do this another day."

"Wait, what?" Krystina asked with a mix of confusion and incredulity. "What do you mean?"

"Things aren't working today, okay?" I snapped, failing to hide my irritation this time.

Pulling free from my arm, Krystina ripped the blindfold off her face before I could stop her. I watched her eyes widen as her vision adjusted to take in our surroundings. It didn't look like much when it wasn't lit up, but I was sure she got the idea.

"Alex, what is all of this?"

"It's nothing now. The lights aren't working for some reason."

My fists clenched and unclenched at my sides, thoroughly disappointed and angry that things were not going as planned. Glancing down, I bent to pick up a small rock and side-armed it into the pond. It made a brief splash before disappearing beneath the surface when it hit the water.

"Why aren't the lights working?" she asked.

"I'm not sure. I plugged them in and got nada. Hale checked the breakers, and all is good there too."

To my surprise, Krystina began to giggle.

"Awww. Are you having a Clark Griswold moment?"

"Who is that?"

"You know. From *Christmas Vacation*. At least we don't have flying squirrels!" she joked.

My eyebrows pushed up in confusion. "I'm sorry— flying squirrels?"

"Yeah! You know the part when Clark is standing by the tree, then Aunt Bethany hears a squeaking sound and —" she stopped short, shook her head, and laughed. "Never mind. I thought I'd made progress on your movie knowledge, but I guess I missed this one. I'll have to add it to the list. Cousin Eddie is must-see TV."

"I'm glad you find this amusing," I said dryly. Krystina's pop culture knowledge far surpassed mine—a fact she loved to remind of and relished the experience of educating me. Sometimes I enjoyed it, other times it was torture. Somehow, I thought any character named Cousin Eddie would fall under the latter.

"Okay, I'm sorry. I won't tease anymore," she said. "But seriously, why do all of this? I mean, most people decorate the front of their houses. Nobody can even see this."

"I don't care about everyone else. I did this for you. I've been working on it for the past few days. You love Christmas so much—especially seeing all the decorations in the city. But you know why I don't want you venturing down to Rockefeller Center. There are just too many people. So while I know this isn't the same, it was my way of bringing the extravagant decorations to you. If you're feeling down about being stuck in the house, I thought this could be a little escape."

"You did all of this for me? As in—you did it all yourself?"

Picking up another rock, I skipped it across the water. I threw it with less venom this time, as feelings of disappointment were beginning to dwarf my anger.

"Sort of. Hale helped me with it," I told her. I pointed to our left toward a clear dome bubble tent. "Do you see that over there?"

"Yes. What is it?"

"It's a garden igloo. I thought we could spend Christmas Eve out here, under the stars with all the lights around us. It will be warm enough inside that we won't have to worry about the cold. I also spoke to Vivian about it. She said she would figure out a way to serve us dinner there if we wanted. And—" I stilled when I saw Krystina's lip quiver and her eyes suddenly fill with tears. "What's wrong?"

"I'm sorry, Alex. I don't mean to cry," she said through a sniffle. Her gloved hands twisted together in front of her, a tell-tale sign that she was anxious or nervous about something as she looked at me through glassy eyes. "Even though the lights aren't working right now, I know what you're trying to do, and I appreciate it so much. In fact, my heart wants to burst just from knowing how much you care."

"I sense a 'but' in there somewhere," I said hesitantly.

"Hearing you talk about spending Christmas Eve out here—with just the two of us—was another reminder that Christmas won't be the same." She rested her hand on my arm. "I just really miss my friends and family, you know?"

Her eyes were pleading, practically begging me to understand. Although she was clearly trying to keep her tone even, she couldn't mask the wistfulness in her voice. It made the disappointment of the failing lights ten times worse.

What I'd done here wasn't enough. It would never be enough.

"I know what you want, Krystina. I'm just doing my best to try and find a balance," I said with agitation. Bending over, I picked up another rock.

"Wait!" Krystina exclaimed and took my hand. Uncurling my fingers, she looked down at the rock in my hand. "Don't throw this one. It's a wishing stone."

"What the hell is a wishing stone?" I asked a little too harshly with an impatient shake of my head.

"A wishing stone is a rock with an unbroken stripe all the way around it. Look here," she said. Removing her gloves, she shoved them in her pocket and began tracing her finger around the rock to show the perfectly unbroken pale quartz ring. "There's no beginning and no end. If you make a wish for yourself when holding the stone, it's supposed to come true. But if you make a wish for someone else, both of your wishes come true."

I wasn't a believer in superstitions, but there was something about the look on Krystina's face that made me pause. The air seemed to stir as I studied her. She was the reason no more shadows or nightmares haunted me. She was my very own angel—the light in my darkness—the woman who helped chase away my demons and dared me to dream.

If I had one wish this Christmas, it would be to give her what she wanted. Yes, she spoke about wanting her friends and family, but I knew what was in her heart. She desperately wanted a baby more than anything else. It was what I wanted too.

Perhaps if we both wished for it...

I shook my head, unable to believe I was considering such nonsense. Krystina had clearly been rubbing off on me too much. Still, I couldn't help but humor her.

Wrapping my hand over hers, I pressed the stone between each of our palms. "Make a wish, angel."

"Together," she said with a smile.

I watched her close her eyes, then I followed suit and made my wish. I nearly laughed at the ludicrous idea that this would make one bit of difference in the outcome of us having a baby. But then I found myself shivering against a cold breeze. The wind kicked up, whipping around us and puffing up billows of snow under the stars.

"Did you feel that?" she whispered.

I opened my eyes to look at her once more.

"The wind?" I asked.

"Yes. The wind that came at the exact moment we made our wish. It was like magic."

My mouth tilted up in amusement.

"Christmas magic? Or maybe it was the Ghost of Christmas Past?"

"Are you making fun of me?" She pushed her lip out in a fake pout.

"Not at all, Mrs. Stone. I think it's sexy when you talk about magic. It makes me want to create some magic of our own."

"Is that so?"

Without answering, I leaned in closer and brushed my mouth against hers. Pushing my tongue past her lips, our kiss deepened, turning breathy and intense in an instant. It was always that way with us. The softest of kisses could ignite into a red-hot flame in the blink of an eye. Despite our differences and many mistakes along the road, Krystina and I never failed at passion.

Her body relaxed against mine, and I felt her submission on a molecular level, stirring every cell in my body to take her right here. I loved this woman with every fiber of my being. She was perfect from the inside out— from her unwavering inner strength right down to the perfect shape of her lips.

And she was mine—all mine.

"We're going to screw in the snow, aren't we?" she whispered against my lips.

I low chuckle reverberated in my chest as I moved my mouth along the line of her jaw.

"Angel, if I weren't worried about you freezing to death, I might consider it."

Pulling abruptly away, I bent down and swooped her up from behind her knees. She laughed, breathless from our kiss, and swatted my shoulder as I cradled her to my chest.

"Put me down, you neanderthal."

"Not a chance—at least not until we get to our bedroom where I can strip you out of your clothes without worrying about you freezing to death."

"Hmmm.... strip me down, huh? What else are you going to do? Drag me across the room by my hair like the caveman I know you to be?"

"Possibly. There may be handcuffs and a paddle, too, if you keep calling me names," I teased.

She flashed me a devilish smile.

"I'll take all of the above, please."

12

Krystina

As Alexander and I made our way back to the house, the sexual tension was palpable. Eventually, he put me down so we could walk at a more hurried pace. Rather than casually strolling like we had when we initially walked down to the pond, we nearly ran back to the house. It was as if neither of us could wait to be naked in each other's arms and were fighting the urge to sprint. I regretted not taking a golf cart, one of the many recreational vehicles kept in the garages. While the path to the pond was easily walkable, the other thirty-six acres of land wasn't as easy to navigate, so golf carts and ATVs were often used to get around. If we'd taken one down to the pond today, we would have made it back to the house so much faster.

When we finally made our way around to the front entrance to the house, I could see that the automatic timers had lit the Christmas tree in the center of the foyer, as well as the lighted garland draped over the front door and exterior windows. The house had a festive glow, but I was feeling anything but festive at the moment. I was only focused on one thing—Alexander. My body hummed with anticipation. No matter what he did, my husband never failed to make me feel electric.

Once inside, Alexander slammed the front door closed unnecessarily hard, then spun to push me roughly against the back of it. His whisper of a smile made my heart skip a beat, and then all at once, his hands were everywhere. Within seconds, he had shed all the winter gear from my body until I was down to my long-sleeved t-shirt and jeans.

My hands flung up to grip the wavy strands of his nearly jet-black hair, needing to pull him closer. I was desperate. It was as if I couldn't get enough. And for me—I would never feel like I'd had enough of this man.

Grabbing my right leg, he brought it up to scissor around his hip, then captured my mouth in a frenzy of gasps. Our hungry tongues collided at a feverish pace as he pressed his groin against me. I moaned from the friction he created against my pulsing heat. I was already lost in him, and I never wanted to find my way back.

Tearing his mouth from mine, he leaned in close to my ear and whispered, "I want you naked and kneeling."

My body quivered from the sound of his voice, itching to obey.

"I'll need a minute to freshen up."

"Be quick about it. No more than fifteen minutes."

"Okay. Then where do you want me? Bedroom or the playroom?" I asked breathily, hoping for the latter.

With a shake of his finger, he tsked at me.

"Don't push me, angel. You know my answer will be the bedroom. I'll meet you there momentarily."

I nodded, brushing off the disappointment that we still weren't going to the playroom, then hurried up the grand staircase to get ready for my insatiable husband. Moving quickly to the bathroom, I stripped down and stepped into our large glass shower to give my legs and lady parts a quick shave. I hadn't shaved that morning, and if there was one thing Alexander loved, it was smooth skin.

After making quick work in the shower, I slathered on a light-scented lotion and was kneeling at the foot of our four-poster bed in record time. It wasn't the same bed that we shared at the penthouse. That one, with its metal framework and hidden saltire cross, had been relegated to the playroom. It was a decision Alexander and I had made when we decided to start a family, thinking it was best to keep the more obvious kink out of plain sight.

However, that didn't mean that the bed sitting in the

middle of our bedroom was ordinary. Oh, no. My husband made sure our new bed was fashioned to his liking—and that included several clandestine loops on the underside so he could easily tie me up good and tight. I couldn't help but wonder if that was on the menu tonight.

My heart pounded in anticipation as I waited in the dimly lit room for him to arrive. Naked and on my knees, the suspense that came from having to wait was an intoxicating turn-on. I wasn't sure how much time had passed—minutes or an hour—but when Alexander finally entered the bedroom, I was dripping with arousal.

I peered at him through lowered lids. He was completely naked, a six feet tall package of male perfection stalking toward me like a predator pursuing his prey. The power of his lean, muscular body was unmistakable. He stopped three feet before me, taking the time to drink in every inch of my body. He circled the place where I knelt, and dark energy hummed in the air.

"What should I do with you, Mrs. Stone?"

His voice was firm and controlled, but I kept my head down and didn't answer, knowing he didn't need one. Right now, all I needed to do was wait for instruction. While we'd had plenty of vanilla sex over the years, domination was what Alexander craved above anything else—and I was more than happy to give it to him. My body was always his for the taking. All he had to do was tell me to be naked and kneeling for me to know he needed my submission. Tonight, I was here at his pleasure. Nothing more.

He stopped behind me and bent to trace a finger from the base of my neck down my spine. Stopping when he reached the crack of my ass, he pulled back, then gave the top of my right cheek a sharp slap. I hissed in a breath from the unexpected sting, but I didn't move. This was only the beginning.

Moving back around to my front, he hauled me to my feet. Splaying his fingers around the back of my head, he gripped the roots of my hair while the other hand kept a firm hold on my jaw. Tilting my head back, he forced my gaze to meet his, then pressed his mouth on mine.

He played for a while, nipping and sucking on my bottom lip before drawing it in between his teeth. He bit down hard, his action meant to cause pain, but not so hard that he'd draw blood. Then, when he'd had his fill, he plunged his tongue into my mouth to take more of what he desired.

Our kiss was wild, mashing at a frenzied pace—attacking, thrusting, tasting, devouring until I began to feel the vibration of his moans against my lips. The sound of his pleasure propelled me to a euphoric state of lust. And when he finally tore his mouth from mine, intense smoldering blue eyes met mine.

"Turn around," he ordered.

I did as he instructed, allowing him to pull my arms behind my back as I spun. His hands tightened around my wrists to show his authority, triggering that part of me that forced my whole body to surrender. It wasn't long before I felt the familiar texture of a silk rope being tied around my wrists. After securing the knot, Alexander leaned in and rimmed the shell of my ear with his tongue before nudging me toward the bed.

"Sit on the edge but don't slide back," he instructed.

Once again, I obeyed his command without question. Once I was seated, he pushed my knees apart and stepped between my thighs. Gliding a finger between my legs, he found my opening and slid through my wet heat. He plunged in up to the second knuckle and began to flick rapidly against my walls.

"Oh!" I gasped.

He added another finger, pushing deeper, and my pulsating muscles tightened around him. With an agonizingly slow twisting motion, he massaged the pleasure spot deep in my core until I was writhing under his palm.

"Be still," he ordered.

I stopped moving but found myself stifling a moan when Alexander moved to kneel between my legs. Cruelly ripping his fingers from the clutches of my body before I experienced release, he shoved me backward. My back arched over my balled fists at the base of my spine until my shoulders kissed the satin sheets beneath me. Then he slid his hands slowly over my calves, spreading my knees wide. I knew what was coming next. He wanted to torture me, knowing it was near impossible for me to be still while he went down on me.

"I want to taste your sweet pussy," he told me, causing my nerve endings to tingle with delight.

Grabbing my legs, he lifted them until they were dangling off his shoulders, then brought his hands back to my center to part my folds with two fingers. With my desire exposed, I pushed up my hips in longing, just waiting for that first flick of his tongue.

When I finally felt him sweep up my entrance and over my clit, I released the moan I'd been holding in. He began lightly, teasing me almost, as he nipped and sucked along my tender flesh. My hands flexed behind my back as every muscle in my body shuddered. I knew I was supposed to be still, but it was near impossible not to pump my hips against his ruthless mouth. I was close. So close.

However, Alexander didn't bring me to climax, but instead pulled his mouth from my body and stood up.

"Turn around. Lay face down on the bed with your legs hanging over the edge."

My stomach tightened, and I nearly came on the spot from the sheer knowledge that this position could mean any number of things. As I shifted into position, my imagination ran wild. Curiosity got the best of me, and I angled my head so I could glance back to see what he was doing. What I saw was a glorious sight to behold.

Alexander stood about five feet away, his eyes focused

on my exposed ass. He was fisting his cock, stroking it languidly from root to tip. Seeing him pleasure himself was always a turn-on for me, and today was no different. There was just something about seeing my alpha husband with his chiseled abs and tight jaw flexing his knuckles around his erection. It caused my inner muscles to spasm in the most titillating way.

The tightening in my belly intensified, the need to feel him all-consuming. With my feet planted firmly on the floor, I pushed my pelvis against the bed, desperate to get some relief.

"Do you want something, angel?" he teased, his voice sounding deep and throaty.

"Yes, please. Alex, I need to feel you," I pleaded.

Much to my satisfaction, he didn't make me wait much longer. Stepping up to me, he positioned his erection at my entrance. The hard tip pushed through my opening, stretching and filling me to completion. The penetration from behind felt impossibly deep, and my immediate cry of pleasure was palpable.

"I don't want you to come. This is for me. You'll have your turn," he warned, then began to move inside me.

He was neither soft nor gentle, chasing his pleasure with relentless force. I sighed when he pressed the flat of his thumb against my puckered rear, holding firmly without penetration as he repeatedly drove into me. His movements were wild and electric, causing something inside me to build until my gaze began to shimmer from the pressure.

"I'm so close!" I panted in between his merciless thrusts.

"Do not come," he ordered again.

"But I—" I stopped short when his hand came down hard against my ass, reminding me that this was all for him. He was in charge, and I was nothing but a slave to his every whim. When he slapped me again, I nearly came on the spot.

Damn him! I'm not going to be able to hold out much longer.

Desperation coursed through my veins. It was the most electrifying aphrodisiac imaginable.

Leaning down, he snaked his hands under my body to cup my breasts and pinch my nipples hard. Sharp, delicious pain ricocheted through me, threatening to send me over hard and fast. He was testing me, deliberately not giving me a moment to prepare. I cried out, fighting against the convulsing need that wanted to overtake me as Alexander began thrusting harder.

God, he's so deep. So deep. Shit.

I clenched my teeth, my head thrashing from side to side, as a tingling sensation spread to my limbs. I couldn't stop it if I tried. Alexander must have sensed how close I was to eruption because he stopped pumping to lean in and whisper, "Did I give you permission?"

"No," I replied through labored breaths.

"Don't come," he repeated, then began to move inside me once more.

This time, his thrusts were more aggressive, pounding into me like a savage beast who cared about nothing else but satiating his lust. And I loved it—loved every minute of his brutal dominance.

His fingers continued to pull and pinch at my nipples before finally releasing my breasts to move to my hips. His grip was firm—bruising almost—and I knew he was close. His fingers dug into my flesh, signaling that it would only be a matter of seconds before I would feel his cock swelling. He pushed impossibly deeper, filling what little space was left inside of me. I bit down hard on my lower lip until I tasted blood, the struggle to keep my own orgasm at bay almost devastating.

"Fuck, Krystina. I..." He trailed off, his guttural tone falling silent as his erection began to pulsate. I stilled, holding on tight to my orgasm and allowing myself to feel every delicious sensation of his seed bursting forth.

13

Alexander

I gave myself a moment to catch my breath before pulling out, and when I finally did, Krystina released a tiny gasp of shock. She was trembling, desperate for the release I'd denied her.

Don't worry, angel. Your turn is coming.

Standing at the edge of the bed, I untied the rope at her wrists. She remained still, but her breaths were labored, and I knew her arousal was near combustion. I'd deliberately pushed her to her limits, knowing just how close to the edge she was. Nevertheless, her irrevocable submission, allowing me to take what I wanted without question, was a beautiful thing, and she deserved worshipping for the rest of the night.

After I finished untying her wrists, I drank in the sight of her draped over the edge of the bed. Krystina regularly exercised in our home gym, and the evidence of her efforts showed in every line of her body. Her seductive curves were all muscle and soft skin. She was exquisite, and she was all mine for the taking.

I ran my fingertip down her spine, stopping at the curve of her ass. I noticed the red outline of my palm on her right cheek from where I'd smacked her. As she lay there patiently waiting for my next instruction, I slowly ran my hand over it, my fingers twitching to give her a matching palmprint on the other side.

What shall I do with you next?

I glanced at the moveable bookcase that hid the staircase to our playroom and contemplated whether I should order her to go there. I knew it was what she wanted. Hell, it was what *I* wanted.

Pressing my lips together, I briefly considered my options, but it didn't take me long to decide that we would not be going to the playroom. She may not be pregnant, but I just couldn't chance the possibility that she might be —not after what happened the last time. It didn't matter how bad I wanted to see her naked body chained and begging. I was observant, and I'd noticed the recent changes to her body. They were subtle, but they were there. I had every line of Krystina's body memorized, and her fuller than normal breasts and slightly swollen labia could be a sign that she was pregnant but didn't know it yet.

I silently cursed myself for not paying attention to her monthly cycle, but as long as I was unsure, there were safer options that didn't require the use of the playroom. Fortunately, there was a toy lying in wait in my nightstand for such an occasion.

"Move up onto the bed so your head is on the pillows," I told her. "Then spread your legs, angel. I want you open to me. I have a surprise that you'll enjoy."

"A surprise?" she questioned, but it sounded more like a seductive murmur as she rolled onto her back. She looked up at me. Her cheeks were flushed, and her eyes were like molten fire. That look was like an electric shock straight to my groin.

"I love how you look when you're flushed from sex. So fucking gorgeous," I growled, fighting the urge to mount her like some kind of savage beast. "Before the night is over, I will have tasted every inch of you. No part will be left unexplored."

Almost instantly, I heard her already labored breathing increase, and I smiled in satisfaction.

Once she was positioned up on the bed, I stepped over to the nightstand to retrieve a small oval-shaped vibrating bullet from the drawer, then climbed onto the bed and crawled over her delectable body. Capturing a nipple between my teeth, I nipped and suckled on the sensitive flesh before trailing hot, wet kisses over her stomach and the curve of her hips. I continued south until my head was between her legs, and I could train my gaze on her beautiful, pink sex. A sheen of moisture, a mixture of her arousal and my seed, glistened on her smooth folds.

I inhaled and groaned. She smelled divine—like sex and sin and everything that was Krystina. Unable to resist, I traced the line of her small opening with my finger. She was dripping with desire.

"Alex..." she whimpered.

Her plea sounded desperate. I knew it would take very little to get her off, but I wanted to take my time with her. I continued to stroke and prod until she began to tremble. I grazed the inside of her thighs with my teeth and inhaled deeply to take in her scent, then parted her lips and blew softly over her clit. When I grazed my tongue over it, she nearly bucked off the bed.

"Do you want to come?" I asked, deliberately taunting her with another tiny flick.

"God, yes. Please, Alex."

"Alright, angel. I'll let you come. I want you to relax your body, let your knees fall apart, and just feel. Are you ready?"

"Yes," she breathed.

Reaching to my left, I grabbed the silver bullet I'd taken from the nightstand. Using my free hand to part her lips, I inserted the cool object into her moist heat. Then, without giving her a moment to react, I flipped the tiny switch to activate the vibrator, shoved her legs further apart, and pressed my tongue to her pulsating bundle of nerves.

Her screams of pleasure were instant. Gripping her hips firmly to hold her still, I ate her like a starving man, relentless in my pursuit of her pleasure. I'd never get enough of her taste. Her scent. Her heat. As she came over the vibrating bullet and into my mouth, I thrust my tongue into her well of honey and drank from her. Her needy cries filled the room as her channel fluttered from the onslaught of my tongue. I wanted to swallow every last drop of her desire and not waste any of it.

She pushed her pelvis against my mouth and pulled at my hair, jerking and moaning as she tossed her head from side to side. A groan escaped me, and I wanted nothing more than to bury myself in her fiery heat once again. My cock twitched anxiously, ready to claim her.

"That's it, angel. You deserved that, but I'm not done with you yet," I told her. "Put your arms above your head. Hang on to the rails of the headboard, and don't let go."

With the vibrating bullet still on and inside of her, I curved my index finger and pushed it inside her soaking wet heat. I teased her for a moment, rubbing against her G-spot and twisting to slather my finger with her moisture. Then, pulling it out, I prodded her puckered rear hole for a moment before plunging into her succulent ass.

Her body twisted in pleasure, but being the good girl

that I'd taught her to be, her arms never moved from above her head. I worked her over with a litany of sensations—tongue, vibrator, finger. I hit all her pleasure points until her cries became frantic and I couldn't tell the difference between a prayer and a curse.

When her second orgasm hit, she came hard and violent, her body bucking and trembling from the impact. Pulling back, I removed my finger and the vibrating bullet from the clutches of the body, then climbed up her to take her mouth fully.

Our tongues mashed, our saliva mixing with the tangy juices of our ecstasy. I trailed open-mouthed kisses over her jaw, nipped at her earlobe with my teeth, and sucked on her neck and the curve of her shoulders. When I began to suckle the soft skin around the peak of her areola, her back arched as she searched for more.

"Do you want to be fucked again, Krystina?"

"Yes, please," she rasped.

"I'll fuck you every way imaginable if that's what you want," I assured her. "But first, I want you to touch me. You can let go of the headboard now."

She didn't need further prompting. In an instant, Krystina's hands were everywhere. Her fingers plunged into my hair, then clawed up and down my back, scoring at my flesh. She gripped my hips, then reached between us to wrap her delicate fingers around my cock. She tugged at the hard member, and I released a hiss of pleasure as her thumb tested the tip for precome. When she found it, she massaged the moisture into my length as her other hand applied pressure to my heavy sack.

My eyes never left her smoldering gaze as she continued to explore my body. She pumped my cock over and over again, her hips rising and falling with the motion of her hand. Then, widening her legs, she positioned my rigid member against her clit and began to rub against me. Her slick pussy was hot as she pleasured herself, and I moaned from the feel of her wet heat.

When her breathing became erratic, I knew she was close to climaxing again.

"That's it, angel. Let me see you make yourself come."

"When I come again, I want you inside me. Please, Alex," she begged breathlessly.

Pulling back, her heavy-lidded eyes locked with mine. Restraint wasn't an option. I had no will to deny her intrepid plea. Without waiting another moment, I grabbed her hands and pinned them down on each side of her head. Gripping her wrists tightly, I plunged into her molten heat and gave her what she craved.

I pushed deep into her, penetrating with aggression and burying myself until there was no way to tell where our bodies began and ended. Her wrists twisted in my grasp, fingers clawing at what little sheet she could find as she tried to find purchase.

We were one, two halves of a soul that could never be complete without the other. She was mine, and only mine, forever. It was only us and the legacy we would create. So when my orgasm finally burst forth in my final thrusts, I silently begged her womb to accept my seed, desperate to one day see her body swollen with my child.

KRYSTINA LAY flaccid in the crook of my arm as our rapid heartbeats returned to a normal rhythm. She had one arm arched over her head while I ran a finger back and forth between her hipbones. Our skin was damp with sweat, but I was still able to appreciate how soft her skin felt.

"Alex, I was thinking about something," she said, shifting to prop her head up on one hand. Her expression was coy, and it caused a low rumble of laughter to escape me.

"I know that look, angel. What do you want?"

"Nothing, really. Well, sort of. I was just thinking about your worries regarding the playroom. You view it as a hard limit, and I will respect that, but you know we don't always have to do strenuous things in there. Right?"

I frowned as I tried to understand why she was pushing to use the playroom so much. She knew my concerns, and she seemed to understand my reasoning when I first told her.

"I don't know what you're trying to get at. I already told you the reason—"

"Yes, yes. I know, and we don't need to rehash it because now it only makes me think about what happened the next day. Until you drew the connection for me, it never used to, but that's not why I brought this up. I just don't see why we can't bring what we just did here, in the bedroom, to the playroom. Then maybe add a bit more kink."

"Are you unsatisfied with our sex life?"

"Oh, god! Of course not!" she said hurriedly with a shake of her head. "I just worry that... well...."

I angled my head and furrowed my brow, curious over her hesitation.

"Go on," I prompted.

"I don't want you to get bored with vanilla—get bored with me."

This time, I really did laugh but pulled her tight to my chest to make sure she knew I wasn't laughing at her. I just found the absurdity of her worry to be comical.

"Angel, I could never be bored with you. I just don't trust myself to be as careful as I need to be with you when we're in the heat of the moment."

"I don't understand."

"It's hard to explain. Controlling you in the playroom is like having every one of my fantasies come true. A whole combination of things can bring the devil in me to life—your willingness to submit, the texture of the leather flogger, the sound it makes when it hits your skin, seeing your rosy flesh, the heavy smell of sex in the air, the adrenaline rush." I paused momentarily when I heard her sudden intake of breath, knowing she was imaging everything I was saying. I pictured it too. It made my cock twitch with anticipation, but I forced myself to continue on. It was imperative that she understood why we could not go to the playroom anytime soon. "All of it makes me want to rule you—to own you. Sometimes, my desire to see your flesh turn a beautiful shade of red is overwhelming, and I lose track of all time and space, solely focusing on the task at hand. So while I'm careful not to push you too far, you know how the lines can sometimes blur. It's why you have a safe word."

"I've never had to use the word sapphire when we were together that way, Alex. I trust you. But I know how important it is for you to experience dominance sexually, and I worry that you aren't getting what you need when we're together."

"It doesn't matter if you trust me when I don't trust myself. Not now—not when there's a chance you could be pregnant. As for me getting what I need, whether it be vanilla or sex with all the kinky bells and whistles known to man—it's you I will always want. If anything, I should be the one expressing worry after the way you've continued to bring up the playroom as of late. Are you sure that *you* are not the one getting bored with me?"

"Don't be silly," she said with a playful swat to my chest.

"I love you, angel. I want nothing more than to make sure you are always far from harm—even if that includes me sometimes."

Pressing her lips into a tight line, she drew her brows together and frowned.

"Speaking of keeping me out of harm's way, there is something else I had to ask you," she added, albeit hesitantly. Her apprehension had alarms bells sounding in my head.

"Why do I get the feeling that I'm not going to like what you're about to say?"

"Just hear me out, Alex. All of this stuff with Stone's Hope has everyone in a tizzy."

"What do you mean by 'in a tizzy' and who is everyone?"

"The entire staff is threatening to quit because we had to cancel the Christmas party for the moms and kids."

"That's ridiculous," I scoffed. "How will a mass exodus help anyone?"

"Well, they think we can and should do more to help them. They're right, even if they don't understand the legal concerns. That said, I came up with an idea. Turning Stone Advertising has no affiliation with Stone Enterprise anymore since I was able to meet the buy out, so I will donate under the advertising business's name. I've already cleared it with Stephen. He doesn't foresee an issue with it."

"If Stephen gave you the all-clear, then I don't see why not."

"Good. So you'll be okay if I stop into the shelter to tell them myself?"

Sitting straight up, I twisted to stare down at her, feeling shocked that she would even suggest such a thing after the lengths we'd gone to keep her isolated.

"Are you out of your mind? Absolutely not! There is no way in hell that I'd allow you to ever step foot into a high-risk congregate setting," I boomed.

"Allow me?" she challenged with raised brows.

"Don't push me, Krystina. This is not the time to pull the independent woman card on me. The answer is no. It's too risky."

"Alex, I really think it will make a difference to the staff if I go. Everyone is just so tired after the past year couple of years. They need a morale boost, and I think I can give it to them."

"Have Justine do it," I countered.

"Justine has enough on her plate with the other areas of the foundation. Besides, I'm not going to have her talk to them about a donation coming from *my* company. That's absurd."

It certainly was absurd, but it didn't matter to me. There was no way I would sanction a visit to a large group setting. The shelter was one of the worst places she could be at a time like this.

"Then do it via video conference. Either way, you're not going to the shelter in person," I said forcefully.

"Alex, you're being unreason—"

"Enough. This isn't up for negotiation. Go to sleep now, Krystina."

"Not until we talk about this."

"I said that's enough!"

I laid back down, pulled the top sheet and comforter over us, then rolled onto my side. With my back facing her, I'd effectively ended the conversation. I waited in silence, hoping I would soon hear my wife's soft and even breathing signaling that she was asleep. However, after thirty minutes of my silence, all I could hear were her quiet sobs.

14

Krystina

I lay curled up under a plush blanket on the sofa in the family room, the only light coming from the television. The TV was muted with a rerun of the primetime news hour playing on the screen. It was after three in the morning, but I couldn't sleep. My mind was spinning with so many things, and I couldn't shut it off no matter how hard I tried.

To say it was a stressful time would be an understatement. This time of year, it was typical for my workload at Turning Stone Advertising to double, as so many of my clients were pushing holiday sales and the like. However, our strategies had changed and adapted over the past eighteen months, making our already lengthy task list even longer. With so many still working remotely, the number of cars navigating the streets was down and it made billboard advertising much less effective. People were using the internet now more than ever and print subscriptions had seen a sharp decline. As a result, my staff and I had chosen to move our clients to mostly online ads, which also meant long, grueling days of expanding our contacts and virtual presence in areas relevant to client needs that were ever changing.

It was a lot to juggle on its own, but when I tossed in the problems at Stone's Hope, everything seemed overwhelming. The shelter was my responsibility—one that I treasured—but there was no denying how tired I was when Alexander and I finally climbed into bed at night. Most days, we'd have dinner, then retreat to our offices to wrap up any of the days unfinished business, before coming back together to watch an episode of whatever we were currently streaming on Netflix. Too depressed by the news, I'd embraced the 'Netflix and Chill' mentality, using the short hour in the evening to decompress after a long workday. Eventually, it had become routine—one that I appreciated now more than ever.

I absently placed a hand over my stomach, wondering how much my little bundle of joy was attributing to my exhaustion and recent insomnia. I was approaching the end of the first trimester and was starting to feel more optimistic about things. Besides the nausea from the so-called morning sickness, I felt good and had almost told Alexander about the baby when we were out by the pond. But then he'd brought up Christmas, reminding me how much I missed family and friends, and it triggered the waterworks.

My emotional state had been a constant rollercoaster as of late, and I knew my frame of mind had been all wrong. So, in the end, I decided not to tell him. It just didn't feel like the right time. I didn't want any distractions when I finally told him about our baby. I wanted the moment to be perfect.

I inhaled deep and gave in to a good yawn. I took it as a sign that I would probably fall back asleep if I went up to bed. Picking up the television remote, I was about to switch it off but paused when I saw the headline on the bottom of the screen.

NYC Records Zero Cases for the Seventh Day in a Row

What are they talking about?

Surely, they couldn't be referring to the virus. Glancing down at the remote, I unmuted the television to hear the reporting.

"...has recorded its seventh day of no local cases. At today's press conference, the mayor thanked healthcare and public workers, and above all else, New Yorkers for doing everything they could to move past the pandemic. After announcing that there would be no more public restrictions in place, the mayor took the time to speak about congregate care settings, reiterating the need to be vigilant, but has agreed to drop all mandated requirements as of Monday. After nearly two years, New Yorkers breathed a sigh of relief. However, some health care officials warn that we shouldn't drop our guard and disagree with...."

My eyes went wide with shock, barely able to process what I'd heard as a million emotions surged. My hands began to shake. I didn't need to hear the rest. I'd heard enough. Pointing the remote at the TV, I powered it off.

With the room now in complete darkness, I leaned back against the sofa. A part of me was thrilled to hear the great news, but another part of me was absolutely furious.

I'd been betrayed by the person I trusted above all others.

No local cases.

No restrictions.

Mandates dropped.

And Alexander was still keeping me locked up in the house.

My fists clenched as my anger built. Seconds ticked by, eventually turning into minutes until I wasn't sure how long I was sitting there in the dark.

I knew what I was getting into when I married Alexander. There were times when he acted controlling and assuming, but it was balanced with so much love and tenderness. When combined, it made up the man I had come to love, know, and understand. I could even empathize with why he needed to maintain control, but his overreaction to the pandemic had been more extreme than I'd realized.

Alexander's need to control everything—including me —had gone too far.

All this time, I'd been so isolated, unable to see my friends and family, and for what? So he could feel secure with me in a bubble? I knew, and had even argued, about the world seeming to resume normal life, but I hadn't realized exactly how understated that was.

I suppose I only had myself to blame for not knowing. My excuse was that I'd been so busy with work and trying to distract myself from thinking about my isolation that I hadn't taken the time to stay informed. The limited TV programming I watched came from streaming services and it was never news related. I was no longer on social media, as the paparazzi just made it nothing but a headache. Even news notifications had been turned off on my phone, as any sort of update from the outside world was depressing, serving only to remind me of the reason I was locked up in the first place. In a way, I'd indirectly created my kind of own isolation outside of anything Alexander had imposed.

But he knew.

Staying up on current events was crucial to

Alexander's business—there was no way he couldn't have known.

And he never said a word.

"The liar," I hissed through gritted teeth. "How dare he?"

I stood up and began to pace, my fury flowing hot in my veins. As my rage grew, I thought about going upstairs to wake my neurotic husband. I wanted to have it out with him more than anything, but then I thought better of it. Yelling at him would get me nowhere. It would only infuriate him and make him double-down on his argument. The better solution would be to ignore his stupid rules all together and let the chips fall where they may. Short of tying me down, he couldn't *make* me stay in the house.

I pressed my lips together in a frown. The fact that I had no trouble imagining that exact scenario was troublesome. We would need to talk about this with Dr. Tumblin as soon as possible. But until that happened, I had no intention of staying caged up in this house any longer.

First thing in the morning, I would go to Stone's Hope. The shelter needed me, and I'd be damned if I was going to let Alexander keep me from going.

Independent woman card, my ass.

My reasons for going there had nothing to do with my independence and everything to do with what was right. Of course, he would be furious when he found out I went against him, but I'd deal with it later. My more immediate problem was slipping past Vivian and Hale. If they caught wind of me leaving, they would alert Alexander. While I was prepared to go a round with him about this, I didn't want Stone's Hope to be the sacrificial lamb. Going there was too important and I didn't want anything to get in my way.

For tomorrow, I'd need to stay under the radar. After that, there would be no more sneaking around. In fact, I saw a lunch date with Allyson in my very near future.

"And forget this working from home bullshit," I muttered to myself.

There was no doubt in my mind that I would be back in the office on Monday morning. I would be careful, of course, and still take precautions. There was no way I would let my spite jeopardize the baby. I'd need to get with the staff at Turning Stone Advertising to establish office protocols, but I saw no reason why we couldn't go back to semi-normal workdays as long as the risks were low. According to the news, things couldn't get much better.

Smiling to myself, I looked forward to all the ways I would torture my husband with my reclaimed freedom. He would have little choice but to watch me come and go from Cornerstone Tower, stewing on his perch on the fiftieth floor, unable to stop me.

And it would serve him right.

15

Krystina

With my mouth in the shape of an O, I angled closer to the bathroom mirror in the master suite and touched up my lipstick. Standing up straight, I blinked a few times, then took in my reflection. The woman who stared back at me looked nothing short of a nervous wreck. Exasperated, I tossed the lipstick back into my makeup bag.

"You've got this. Everything will be fine," I said to myself. I took a deep breath and moved to the bedroom to make myself comfortable on the settee near the front window. All I could do now was wait with bated breath for the all-clear.

Hale had left hours ago. Considering the number of supplies he needed to get, I didn't expect him to be back until dinnertime. Vivian should be leaving at any minute to pick up the groceries. However, the grocery trip was a short run, and finding a way to keep her away from the house for more than an hour had been a challenge. I ended up starting my day much earlier than usual as a result.

After finishing my work on the Beaumont campaign by eight, I then spent the rest of the morning creating a retail shopping list of items that weren't really needed. I arranged several curbside pickup orders for Vivian at various places just to keep her busy. The orders ranged from clothing stores to Christmas décor suppliers. When I told Vivian about the must-have cashmere sweater I wanted from Saks, she'd eyed me curiously but thankfully didn't question it.

With the added stops I'd given her, she would be out of the house for at least three hours. That would give me plenty of time to drive into the city, talk to Stone's Hope staff, and make it back before Hale or Vivian did. With any luck, Alexander would be none the wiser about my little venture. And if he found out, oh well. I was done living in his gilded cage. I'd thrown the door wide open, and I had no intention of being locked in again. Besides, it was for a good reason. I endured my controlling husband's wrath before, and I'd survive it again if I had to. He never stayed mad at me for long.

Still, my attempt at aloofness did nothing for my nerves. No matter how overbearing I thought Alexander was being, I couldn't ignore the reason he was concerned about my safety in the first place—even if he didn't fully understand how concerned he truly needed to be yet. My bravado from last night had long since disappeared. Yes, I was still angry with my husband, but it had become overshadowed by worry for my unborn baby. If I was going to go through with this, I needed to be extremely careful.

When I saw Vivian's late-model maroon Oldsmobile pull around from the back of the house and disappear down the driveway, I knew the coast was clear. Grabbing a bottle of hand sanitizer and two masks, I made my way downstairs. I knew double masking was over the top, but after listening to Alexander's concerns for months on end, I figured it was better to be safe than sorry. Too much was a stake. With our sad history of failed pregnancies, I didn't want something as simple as an inadequate face covering to put the baby in jeopardy.

Going through the kitchen and out the back door, I headed toward the Porche Cayenne Turbo S parked in the garage, just one of many cars in Alexander's collection. The larger vehicle wasn't my favorite to drive, as I preferred cars that were lower to the ground, but it would be the safest. Heavy snow was in the forecast later on this evening, and the SUV's four-wheel-drive might come in handy just in case it started falling early.

Slipping into the driver's seat, I buckled my seatbelt. My body buzzed with nerves as I backed out of the garage and began the drive toward the city that never sleeps.

LESS THAN AN HOUR LATER, I parked the car and exited the parking ramp located down the block from Stone's Hope. I'd made good time, and I was surprised by the lack of traffic. But even more surprising was the lack of people on the city streets, and I couldn't help but wonder if I'd imagined the news that I'd seen on the television last night. I expected to see more people out and about. Even during the winter months, people were always crowded on the sidewalks, coming and going to or from their homes, places of work, or local businesses.

I also couldn't help but notice how many vacant storefronts I'd passed on my ride in. I hadn't been to the city in over a year, and even though I'd heard the occasional news report about how hard businesses had been impacted by the virus, I'd just assumed their doom and gloom was a bit of an exaggeration. Sadly, it didn't seem to be hyperbole at all, and seeing the desolation firsthand was depressing. This just didn't *feel* like my New York and it angered me to know I'd been so completely in the dark about her suffering—and all because of Alexander's need to control me.

I slipped on my gloves as I climbed from the vehicle.

My hands were shaking, and I wasn't sure if it was from the cold or because I was still so angry at Alexander for lying to me. I walked the three blocks to the shelter, and as I approached the entrance to the building, I glanced up at the sky. Dark, ominous clouds were moving in quicker than I'd anticipated, and I superstitiously crossed my fingers, hoping the worst of the snow would hold out until after I was home.

When I reached the glass front door of the building, I cracked my neck from side to side and tried to shake off the tension. After looping the strings of my masks around each ear, I went inside.

I spotted Claire sitting behind the main reception desk. Even from a distance, I could see how tired she looked. Deep lines and dark circles surrounded her ordinarily bright eyes. Considering the short staff at the shelter, I wasn't sure if she was tired from overwork or the stress from the stolen money.

I glanced around at my surroundings. Behind Claire, two staff members sat typing away on their keyboards in their cubicles. The waiting room was empty, but I couldn't help noticing the wide spaces between the chairs. That's when I saw the large sign taped to the wall.

Please be mindful of our congregate setting.
Social distancing is still in effect for the protection of our guests and staff.
Masks are encouraged but not required.

I felt a slight increase in my pulse when I read masks were optional. It didn't matter if the news I'd watched last night had said as much. Experiencing it firsthand made me feel extremely vulnerable.

I looked around again, checking the faces of everyone I saw. There were several women and children in the common room just down the hall. I could see little boys and girls playing various games through the cordoned-off glass wall. Other than the staff members, very few people wore a mask. This shouldn't make me nervous. After all, there hadn't been any reported cases of the virus in a week.

Still, Alexander's concerns had gotten into my psyche and there was no calming my nerves. My hands twisted in front of me, and I wondered if this was all just a bad idea.

Shoving my fidgeting hands in my coat pockets, I approached the reception desk.

"Can I help you?" Claire asked when I reached her.

"Claire, it's Krystina. Krystina Stone."

"Oh my gosh! I'm sorry. It's been so long since I've seen you, and I didn't recognize you with the mask on," she hurried from her seat behind the desk and came around to greet me.

There was an awkward moment that typically would have been filled with a brief hug, but the shelter's social distancing requirements prevented it. My chest tightened, suddenly realizing how desperate I'd been for human connection outside of my immediate household. Now that I had it, I couldn't even experience it to its fullest.

This is so sad.

I choked back the tears that always seemed at the ready as another wave of melancholy washed over me. Whether Alexander was overreacting or not, things had clearly changed. I wondered if the world would ever be the same again.

"It's so good to see you," I told her in an overly cheery voice, hoping to cut through the sad awkwardness.

"Likewise. I didn't know you'd be stopping in today," Claire said. "I hope your visit means you're here with good news."

"Well, the stop definitely wasn't planned, but I do have something to share with you. First, can you round up the staff and current residents? I'd like to tell everyone at the same time if I can."

"All the residents? Including the kids?"

"Yes. Definitely the kids."

"Sure thing, Mrs. Stone. You can head back to the group therapy room, where there's plenty of space for everyone. I'll tell everyone to gather there."

Claire went to get the other staff members, and I walked down the corridor that led to the large conference room used for group therapy sessions and other large group activities. I was well acquainted with the room, as I'd been a guest speaker several times in the past. It was initially part of my commitment to become more involved with the shelter, but it had turned into so much more. I missed the time that I used to spend here. As much as it hurt to see so many struggling women, the assistance we offered them at Stone's Hope was rewarding enough to get past it. The shelter had been a life-changer for so many, and I was proud to be a part of it.

When I reached the conference room, I saw a large circle of chairs. Every other chair had a red X taped on it, signaling where people were allowed and not allowed to sit. I thought about the number of times I'd seen one woman reach for the hand of another in the group sessions. My heart sank to see how they weren't physically able to do that anymore, and I suddenly had a new appreciation for Claire's frustrations. All of this truly went against human nature and only strengthened my resolve that coming here was the right thing. Stone's Hope needed me—they needed a Christmas—even if it only made them feel normal for a little while. Hopefully, they will feel more of that normalcy after all the mandates drop next week.

Fifteen minutes later, everyone had gathered in the conference room. The limited seating filled up quickly, forcing some staff members and mothers with their children to either sit on the floor or stand along the walls. I took my spot in the middle of the group. Turning in place, I took in the tired and wary looks in the eyes of every mother and the curious expressions of their children.

"Thank you all for taking a few minutes to meet with me," I began. "For those who don't know me, my name is Krystina Stone. My husband, Alexander, is the founder of The Stoneworks Foundation, the non-profit organization that founded Stone's Hope. I'm here today because I have some good news to share. I'm not sure how many of you know about the recent theft we had at Stone's Hope." I paused and saw most everyone nodding.

"Yeah, we know what she did," said one of the mothers. She shook her head in disappointment. Her daughter stood in front of her with wide eyes. She was a tiny thing with bouncy pink ribboned pigtails. She couldn't have been more than four years old. The woman placed her hands on the little girl's shoulders. "It's a damn shame, too. The kids were really looking forward to the party."

"Well, what if I told you that the Christmas party was back on?" I said with a wink.

Several shrieks of excitement came from the kids, but before I could elaborate further, a loud bang from behind me caused me to jump. I turned to see what had caused the noise just as several gasps filled the quiet space. I snapped my attention in the direction everyone seemed to be looking.

Instantly, I brought my hands up to my face, but there

was no way for me to stifle my own gasp of shock. Hannah Wallace, Stone's Hope Christmas thief, stood in the doorway to the conference room with her arms stretched out in front of her. Held tightly in two hands was a gun—a gun that was pointed directly at me.

16

Alexander

I stared absently across my monochromatic office in Cornerstone Tower. The wall of flatscreen televisions were on but with the volume muted, each screen displaying some sort of national coverage. One showed stock tickers, another exhibited the latest political poll numbers, while the third was tuned to a talk show on Bloomberg TV. I barely noticed any of it. I was too consumed with worry over Krystina's odd behavior that morning.

She had acted off—very off.

Yes, she had a situation at Stone's Hope that she was

worried about. I'd listened to her tears long into the night and knew she was upset that I wouldn't allow her to go to the shelter. But it was more than just that. Krystina hadn't seemed quite like herself well before Claire had called her about the stolen money. While I thought our relationship was in a good place, I couldn't help noticing that a strange undercurrent always seemed present. She'd been off for the past couple of months—anxious almost—but it had seemed amplified this morning. I just couldn't put my finger on it. It made me think that something else was bugging her.

I released a frustrated sigh. Krystina was strong, as she had proved time and again, but everyone had their breaking point. I just wish there was some way I could ease her burdens. Other than leaving the office early to go home so she wasn't alone quite so much, my hands were tied. I had no control over too many things that were affecting my wife—and it was driving me fucking crazy.

I glanced down at the printout of my daily calendar that Laura had left on my desk this morning. I contemplated leaving early again today, but my day was full. I had contracts to review, and I couldn't rearrange any of my meetings. I flipped the page to see what was on the schedule for next week. It was clear that skating out of work early a few times a week was starting to catch up with me. My schedule appeared jam-packed straight through to Christmas Eve.

"Dammit."

I couldn't be working until seven every night. This schedule would never work if I wanted to ensure Krystina's mental well-being was the priority. I would need to shift some of the appointments to the following week.

Opening the top drawer of my desk, I rifled around for a highlighter to mark which appointments I would need Laura to move. In my search, I came across a square invitation to the Governors Charity Ball that had somehow gotten shoved to the back of the drawer.

I ran my fingers over the embossed gold lettering and recalled that night more than three years ago. It was an evening for greasing palms and rubbing elbows with the rich and the famous, all under the guise of giving recognition to the underprivileged at thirty-thousand dollars a plate. I had been invited to the dinner because the Andrew Carnegie Medal of Philanthropy was being presented that night, and I was under consideration for the contributions The Stoneworks Foundation had made to the city.

At first, I didn't want to attend. I never liked that kind of recognition because I'd always felt that others were more deserving. However, Krystina had insisted that I go. I was glad I'd conceded, solely because I was able to watch my new wife work a room.

We had been married for less than a year, and she was

still fairly new to black-tie events like the Governors Ball. While she'd been nervous about mingling with celebrities, it didn't take long for her to settle right in. Before the end of the night, she'd managed to snag over three million dollars in donations to help improve conditions in the neighborhood surrounding Stone's Hope. Her logic had been that struggling women didn't want to go into a rundown area to seek help during a time when all they wanted was safety and security for themselves and their children.

The movie stars, politicians, and the press had eaten it up, opening their wallets for a neighborhood revitalization project that New York City hadn't seen in decades. I couldn't even recall who ended up receiving the Medal of Philanthropy that night, as Krystina had been the one to steal the show.

After seeing her in action, I'd asked her to oversee the operations at Stone's Hope. She had wanted to become more involved with the shelter, so saying yes had been an easy decision for her. She loved it, and its success had quickly become a source of pride for her.

However, I was now beginning to wonder if she was juggling too much. My wife never did anything half-fast. She put her heart and soul into everything she did. Perhaps she hadn't seemed like herself lately simply because she was feeling overworked. If that were the case, I would have to consider stepping in.

I pursed my lips and contemplated what I could do, only to realize the answer was simple. All I had to do was tell Justine to step up. After all, my sister was the Head of Operations at The Stoneworks Foundation, and the shelter fell under that umbrella.

Tossing the Governors Ball invitation aside, I reached for my cell phone. But before I could dial Justine's number, the conference phone on my desk buzzed.

"Excuse me, Mr. Stone," my secretary said through the intercom.

"Yes, Laura."

"Hale is on line one."

"Put him through, please."

A moment later, Hale's voice came through the speaker.

"Boss, sorry to bug you."

"It's fine, Hale. What's up?"

"A few things. First, I just got off the phone with Liz Schiller from Public Relations."

My jaw clenched. Hale talking to anyone from my PR team was rarely a good thing.

"What did she have to say?" I asked.

"Apparently, Mac Owens has been sniffing around. She's concerned because of that picture someone snapped of Krystina by the pool a few years ago, and she just wanted to make sure I tightened security on the property."

My fists tightened at the mention of the reporter from

The City Times. I'd worked hard to keep my secrets buried
—especially from the likes of him. He'd been a thorn in
my side for as long as I could remember, but I hadn't
heard his name mentioned in quite a while.

"He's still around? He's always been too damn
suspicious about everything. Why would he be poking
around my business again?"

"It's about Krystina. There hasn't been a picture of her
in public in nearly two years."

"So what? We've been in a global pandemic."

"True. But with much of the world back to normal for
months now, he wanted to know why Krystina hasn't been
seen out and about."

"It's none of his damn business," I quipped.

"I know that, but you know how the paparazzi love to
stalk her. If Mac Owens is questioning her whereabouts, it
won't be long before the rest of the vultures decide to
circle. That's why Liz Schiller called to warn me. But
honestly..." Hale paused, and his hesitation was palpable.

"Go on," I prompted.

I heard his sigh on the other end of the line. "With all
due respect, sir, but why hasn't Krystina been out? She
can't be kept caged forever. At some point—"

"Don't cross that line, Hale," I warned, cutting him off
mid-sentence. Hale had never married or had children. I
didn't expect him to understand what I'd felt each and
every time Krystina lost a baby. It was the driving force
behind my need to protect her from harm. "The only

thing you need to worry about are the protocols to keep her safe. Nothing more."

"Fair enough," Hale said, but I heard the skepticism in his tone, and it was goddamned irritating.

"Anything else?" I queried.

"Yeah, two more things. Do you remember the background check we ran on Krystina when you first met?"

"I do, yes."

"When you became serious with her, I branched out to look into other members of her family as well. It was for your protection, sir."

I hadn't realized he'd done that, but when I thought about it, I would've expected nothing less from him. If Hale was nothing else, he was thorough.

"Okay. Why are you bringing this up now?" I asked.

"I've kept tabs on Krystina's biological father."

"Her biological father? Do you know who he is? I don't think Krystina even knows his name. If she does, she's never mentioned it."

"His name is Michael Ketry. I'm bringing this up because he recently moved to the city. His apartment is within walking distance of Cornerstone Tower. It may be nothing, but I find it a little suspect. I'm going to keep an eye on him."

Standing, I crossed the room to the mini bar in my office. It was barely two in the afternoon, but I felt unusually unsettled about what I'd just heard. I may have committed to not drinking alcohol around Krystina while we were trying to get pregnant, but that rule didn't apply when she wasn't here. Taking a tumbler off the shelf, I poured myself a shot of Glenmorangie Grand Vintage Single Malt Whisky.

Looking down at my glass, I swirled the brown liquor for a moment. Raising the tumbler to my lips, I took a sip and contemplated what Hale's news could mean. As he said, it could be nothing, but it could be everything.

"Keep a close watch on this, Hale. I want to know about any developments."

"That goes without question," he assured.

I walked over to the windows. I looked out at the Manhattan skyline and tried to recall what Krystina had told me about her biological father. It wasn't much. She'd referred to him as her sperm donor in passing and said he left when she was just a baby. If he kept tabs on her and found out she was married to me—which was highly likely considering the press's obsession with every move my wife made—he may end up being like every other vulture out there trying to come after my money. While he would never get a cent from me, the upset it could bring was something I didn't want my wife to have to deal with.

"Don't mention this to Krystina, Hale. I don't know why, but I feel this would upset her. His relocation to the city could be harmless. No need to worry her unless there's something more concrete."

"Yes, sir."

"Alright then. What's the last thing you were calling about?"

"It's probably nothing to worry over, but a silent alarm was tripped at Stone's Hope about ten minutes ago. The police are on their way to check things out. They said they'll call me when they get there."

I thought about the building's layout and the state-of-the-art alarm system.

"Which alarm was triggered?"

"The conference room. Someone might have just bumped it during one of the group therapy sessions. It's happened before, but I figured you should know. I'm on my way to the medical supply store on 3rd Avenue, picking up the items the nursing staff wanted for your mother. Assuming traffic is light, I could be at the shelter in about twenty minutes if you want me to check it out."

"No. It's like you said—probably nothing. Keep me updated. I don't have any meetings for the next hour, so you can call my cell directly with any developments. No need to bother Laura."

"Will do."

I ended the connection but paused rather than dial Justine as planned before Hale called. Something didn't feel right, and instinct had me dialing Krystina's cell instead. At the very least, she would want to know there might be something amiss at the shelter.

After the fifth ring, it went to voicemail. Assuming she

was just busy wrapping up her holiday ad deadlines, I left her a message.

"Angel, it's me. Call me when you get this."

After punching the end call button, I began to drum my fingers on the desktop. The seconds ticked by, each one seeming longer than the last. I couldn't shake the feeling that something was wrong—very wrong.

I redialed Krystina's cell, but there was still no answer. My sense of dread grew, so I quickly dialed the landline to the house. The only reason we even had the landline was so that I could get a hold of Vivian. She refused to have a cell phone and, for the first time, I was thankful for my housekeeper's aversion to technology.

When there was no answer at the house, frustration began to set in.

"Damn! Why the hell do we have all of these phone lines if nobody can answer them?" I muttered to myself as I slammed back against the back of my chair. Then a new thought occurred to me.

If nobody is answering the house phone, then perhaps nobody is home. That would mean...

No. She promised. Krystina wouldn't leave the house.

Or would she?

Maybe she just went for a walk outside.

I quickly grabbed my cell to pull up the phone finder app for Krystina. A few minutes later, her location populated on the screen—and she was not just out for a walk. In fact, she was nowhere near our house in Westchester.

She was at Stone's Hope.

What the hell is she doing there?

Before I could even process that my wife had defied me, my cell began to ring. Hale's name showed up on the caller ID.

"Talk to me, Hale. Why the fuck is Krystina at the shelter and not safe at home?"

"She's at the shelter? Stone's Hope shelter?"

"Is there another shelter she'd be at?" I snapped.

"Well, no. It's just that...shit!" Hale cursed, but there was no missing the alarm in his voice.

"It's just what, Hale? What's going on?"

"I just got off the phone with the police. It wasn't a false alarm. There's a hostage situation over there."

All the air seemed to escape my lungs. "A hostage situation?"

"I don't know all the details. The police didn't tell me more than that. I'm headed there now."

Heavy pressure pushed down on my chest, and I began to shake with fury as suppressed memories broke free.

Krystina in a trunk. Bloodied. Broken.

The incessant beep-beep of her bedside monitors in the hospital echoed in my mind, reminding me of her lifeless form and of how I'd almost lost her once before.

"Hale," I choked out, but I didn't need to explain what I was thinking. He understood because he'd been there the last time. He'd been witness to me sitting vigil next to Krystina's hospital bed for nineteen long days after her ex-boyfriend and my deranged ex-brother-in-law had kidnaped her. I couldn't live through that again. Not ever again.

"I'm five minutes away from Cornerstone Tower," Hale said hurriedly. "I'll pick you up at the main doors."

17

Alexander

Time seemed to move in slow motion as Hale weaved in and out of traffic, through the city streets, toward Stone's Hope. During the drive, I had a strange sense of déjà vu—as if Hale and I had been here before. In a way, we had been, and I could only pray the outcome would be different this time, and that Krystina was somehow free from the dangers at the shelter.

A light snow had begun to fall, making the roads slippery and slowing our progress. The forecasters predicted three inches tonight, and I expected it wouldn't be long before the snow became heavier. My fingers drummed impatiently on the door panel as Hale navigated us closer to the shelter.

When the building finally came into view, my heart was pounding in my ears, and the air seemed to buzz. A cold numbness spread through me when I saw the red and blue flashing lights from several police cars blocking the street in front of Stone's Hope.

Hale got as close as he could until he was forced to park. He had barely killed the engine, but I'd already wrenched open the passenger door handle. Jumping out of the car, I rushed toward the shelter.

A metal barricade had been erected to keep the small crowd that had gathered away from the building. Men in uniform gathered near one of the cop cars. I tried to discern what they were doing as I approached, only to conclude that they appeared to be doing nothing— absolutely nothing.

My jaw clenched, instantly furious over their apparent lack of action, as I pushed past the barrier and made my way over to them.

"Excuse me," I said tersely to one of the officers. He turned to face me. Dressed in a traditional navy patrol uniform, he looked young and polished. He was most likely fresh out of the academy because he didn't look a day over twenty-five.

"Sir, please step back behind the barriers. We've got—"

"No," I interrupted. "I own this establishment, and I have reason to believe my wife is inside the building."

The rookie officer paused then, seeming to assess me.

"You're Alexander Stone?"

"That's right."

"I'm Officer Bailey. I've heard of you, but it's nice to meet you in the flesh."

I gritted my teeth, my patience razor thin. There wasn't time for pleasantries.

"Likewise. Now about my wife," I reminded him, desperately trying to remain calm. "Her phone's GPS signal shows she's inside."

"Well, Mr. Stone, if that's the case, then she may be in a bit of trouble. There's a hostile gunman inside," he said nonchalantly.

It was all I could do not to ring the kid's neck. There was nothing blasé about the situation whatsoever.

"A gunman?" I prompted when he didn't elaborate further.

"Well, it's actually a woman. The doors were all locked when we got here, so we tried to call inside. Nobody answered, so we swept the perimeter. That's when we saw a woman through one of the windows. She was waving a gun around and pointing it at a crowd of people."

I looked the officer squarely in the eyes.

"How many people?" I demanded, desperately trying to keep the panic out of my voice. "Did you see a woman with dark brown curly hair, about five feet six inches tall?"

"I can't say for sure."

"What about any demands?" I asked. If it was money the woman wanted, I'd pay anything if it meant my wife would no longer be held at gunpoint.

"We don't know her demands or if there are any. She hasn't reached out. Right now, I need you to calm down while we wait for the Hostage Negotiation Team to get here. They are the ones who will try to make contact. I can't do much else until then. The roads are starting to get slick from the snow, so I'm guessing they'll be here in about fifteen minutes."

My eyes widened in disbelief as rage began to pump hot and fierce through my body. I stepped up the officer until we were toe-to-toe.

"Calm down? Did you just tell me to calm down, officer? My wife is inside, being threatened with a gun, while you just sit around here waiting for someone else to get here to handle the situation? A lot could happen in fifteen minutes!"

"Sir, step back. I understand what you're saying, but I haven't been trained in hostage situations. There are protocols, and none of the officers on scene are authorized to take the next step," he said as if that justified his reasoning for doing nothing.

I turned when I felt Hale's hand on my shoulder. I had no idea when he'd come up behind me, but I knew he sensed I was on the verge of snapping. I didn't know anyone who wouldn't if they were in my shoes. The cop's aloofness to the seriousness of the situation was maddening. I wanted nothing more than to level him.

Shrugging off Hale's hand, I turned back to the officer.

"That's my wife in there, goddammit! What do you mean you're not authorized? You know what? Fuck this and fuck your protocols. I'll figure out how to get inside myself," I growled. I refused to remain helpless in this surreal turn of events.

Suddenly, a horrific crack sounded through the air, causing me and everyone else in the vicinity around to jolt.

A gunshot.

Spinning to face the building, the blood in my veins instantly turned to ice. Without warning, all sense of time seemed to freeze as I was suddenly overcome with memories of my life with Krystina.

Her breathtaking smile on our wedding day.

Her laughter that could brighten the darkest of moments.

Her expressive chocolate brown eyes.

Her touch.

Her fierce determination.

Every moment we'd ever shared seemed to flash before my eyes, choking me until I thought I might suffocate. Just like the snowflakes falling from the sky, she was unique in her own way and I couldn't image a life without her in it.

All rational thought erased from my mind. My mouth

went dry, and my already rapid heartbeat accelerated. I didn't care what the cop was saying. The urge to protect the most important thing in my life was the only thing I could focus on.

Ignoring the protests of the cop, I shoved past him and started toward the building.

"Mr. Stone, wait!" Hale called out.

His cry was echoed by Officer Bailey's and the other nearby cops, but I hurried on undeterred. I couldn't just sit idly by. I had to get to Krystina. She had a terrible habit of making poor decisions that would land her in sticky situations. In hindsight, it was no wonder I was so protective of her. She didn't have the best track record.

She'll be okay. My angel is a survivor.

I repeated that to myself as I hastily moved toward the building. When I was almost to the glass front doors, I felt a hand grab me roughly by the shoulder. I spun, intending to knock out whoever dared to try and stop me, only to find myself face-to-face with three men in navy uniforms.

Before I could react, I was sent hurling face down onto the cold, snow-covered pavement. I struggled to break free as they wrenched my arms behind my back.

"Get off me!" I roared.

The police officers ignored my demand, and as the handcuffs clicked into place, I knew any chance I had of saving Krystina was lost.

18

Krystina

My body shook as I knelt on the ground, face down, with my hands covering my head. Bits of drywall from the ceiling fell around me. Every person in the room had collapsed to the floor when Hannah discharged the weapon. I could hear the quiet whimpers of the children and the soothing whispers from their mothers.

"I'm sorry!" Hannah said hurriedly. "I didn't mean to do that! It-it just went off and-and... I've never used a—" She stopped short and choked on a sob.

I angled my head to peer at her. She held the gun out in front of her, staring at it with apparent shock. Her arms and hands were visibly shaking, and her eyes were as wide as saucers. Even though she had been the one to fire the weapon, Hannah appeared just as scared as the rest of us.

I looked through the glass windows behind her. Although I couldn't see who was out there, I was able to see the flashing lights of police cars signaling that help was nearby. I wasn't sure how they knew there was trouble at the shelter, but that didn't matter as long as they were here.

I turned my head and glanced around the room, hoping to find a weapon of some kind. My quick scan revealed nothing but Christmas decorations. Red, green, and silver garland hung on the walls, and *Hey Santa Claus* could be heard playing quietly from the round speakers in the ceiling. The combination was a stark contrast to the unfolding situation, and I was suddenly reminded of my conversation with Alexander about the movie *Christmas Vacation*. I suspected the song was the reason for the memory trigger, as I tended to relate everything to music. It made me envision a SWAT team busting through the windows to save us all from this hostage situation just like they had in the film.

But then the image of the Griswold's yuppie neighbors being disturbed from their sleep filled my mind. Manic laughter threatened to bubble from my lips as I could not process the absurdity of my line of thought at a time like this. I tamped down feelings of pure hysteria, forcing myself to focus on the crisis at hand.

I needed to do something—anything—to deescalate the situation. My breathing was erratic, the panicked breaths almost suffocating under my double layer of masks. I took a moment to calm my racing heart and allowed self-preservation to take over. Once I felt a bit calmer, I thought about the best ways to protect the baby and me.

Hannah seems scared. Perhaps if I try to appeal to her rational side, she'll see reason.

Raising my hands in the air, I cautiously lifted my head off the ground.

"Hannah, it's me. Krystina," I said, moving ever so slowly to push my masks down so she could see my face.

"I knew it was you. By-by your hair," she stumbled nervously. "I was always jealous of it."

"Thanks, I guess. I've always thought these curls were a bit of a hassle," I said lightly as I gradually moved back to a standing position. "Look, Hannah. It's Christmastime. What do you think about losing the gun so we can talk about this rationally?"

"No!" she said, suddenly seeming to find her courage once again. Then, moving the gun between Claire and me, she said, "Which one of you reported me to the police?"

"Nobody, Hannah. We've been here the whole time," I said.

"No, not today. I'm talking about the money. Who told the police I stole the money?"

"Please. You have to understand. I—" Claire began from her crouched position on the ground.

"I knew it was you! Do you know what's going to happen to me now?" Hannah screeched.

"No, no. It wasn't her. Our accountant found the missing money," I lied, hoping Claire would play along but not daring a sideways glance in her direction. "Now, can you please put the gun down? Talk to me, Hannah."

"I-I can't. You don't understand!"

"So, why don't you tell me?"

"I don't need all these people knowing my business!" Hannah bellowed. "I did what I did, and now I need to do what I need to do to protect my baby girl."

I looked around the room, taking in the terrified gazes of every woman and child. These children didn't need to be subjected to this kind of terror. If I succeeded in nothing else, I had to do something to get them to safety.

"You're right, Hannah," I said. "These people don't need to hear your personal business. Why don't you let all the moms, kids, and the other staff leave? After all, it was my accountant who reported the missing money, so you and I should have a one-on-one to sort this all out."

Her eyes darted wildly around the room, flitting from Claire to me, then back to Claire. It was as if she were trying to weigh her options. Eventually, she jerked her head toward the exit door.

"Go quickly, but you—" she said, angling the gun back at me. "You stay."

Claire scrambled to her feet and began ushering everyone from the room. Hannah's eyes followed each person as they filed out, but she never lowered her weapon. My pulse pounded in my ears, the loud beat quickening as I began to second guess my request for everyone to leave. In a matter of seconds, I'd be all alone with a woman who had a gun trained on my chest.

After everyone was gone, she sidestepped to kick the door closed behind them. The slamming of aluminum against the metal door frame echoed through the room and caused my heart to lurch into my throat. Prowling her way back toward me, she kept the gun level. My racing pulse continued to hammer in my ears, but I refused to take my eyes off her.

Once she reached me, she pressed the barrel just below my breastbone. I sucked in a surprised breath when I felt the tremble of her hand. I knew she was just as terrified as I was, but to physically feel the unsteadiness in her hand made me feel a whole new kind of fear. After unintentionally firing the gun into the ceiling earlier, I knew she wasn't experienced with a loaded weapon. One wrong move, and she could accidentally discharge a bullet into my chest.

I stared directly into her glassy, bloodshot eyes, needing to get a better read on her. Her face was twisted into a sneer, but her eyes were filled with horrendous pain and wild confusion, combined with overwhelming worry and fear. She was trying to be tough, but it was all a façade. My instincts were right. The woman before me was desperate—nothing more. I could talk her down. I was sure of it.

Still, desperate people could be unpredictable, and I would need to tread carefully to protect myself and the baby growing inside of me.

And to think I'd been worried about a virus when I walked through the doors of Stone's Hope. Had I only known...

I glanced down at the cold barrel of the gun. I didn't know squat about guns and had no idea if she managed to put the safety on or if it was still off. I didn't even know what a safety looked like. Then, looking back up to meet her eyes, I angled my chin so as not to show intimidation and focused my eyes on her.

"You mentioned your daughter," I said. "I haven't seen her since the day you first came to the shelter. How is she doing?"

The wildness in her eyes slipped a bit, revealing a deep level of sadness.

"She's good. Eva is... she's so beautiful and so smart," Hannah said wistfully. She sniffled and tried to blink back the tears that had begun to well in her eyes. "She's only four years old, but she can already read. Unfortunately, I can't afford pre-school, and I had to teach her so she's ready for kindergarten next year."

"That's amazing! What else has Eva been up to?" I

asked, needing to keep her talking. I hoped if I stalled long enough, help would eventually come.

"She eats a lot."

What an odd thing to say.

"Oh, is that right?" was my only reply, but when she spoke again, the reason for her statement became clear.

"It's why I took the money. I needed to feed her. And don't give me a lecture about the help that's available— you—living in that big fancy house. I saw pictures of it on the news. People like you have no idea what it's like to be in my shoes," she pointed out bitterly.

"You're right. I don't, and I won't pretend to understand. But I can empathize and listen. Tell me about your struggles, Hannah. Maybe I can do something to help."

"There's nothing you can do."

"Try me."

"Do you have kids?"

"No, but..." I trailed off, eyeing the end of the gun as I slowly moved my arms to place both hands over my abdomen. "I don't have any now, but I have one on the way."

"You're pregnant?" she asked with surprise.

"Yes, but don't tell anyone. It's a secret," I said conspiratorially, hoping to gain her trust just enough for her to point the gun somewhere else.

"Well, you'll learn soon enough. Kids need things that you can't always give them. But you're lucky. At least you have the baby's daddy around to help—and he's loaded. Eva's father has been in and out of prison so many times that it's been mostly just her and me for a long time. It's been hard. Real hard."

"I'm sure it has been," I sympathized, hoping my tone would encourage her to keep talking. I chanced a quick glance at the windows but still only saw the flashing lights of police cars from somewhere nearby.

What's taking them so long to come in here? Claire had to have let them in by now. Or maybe the police lights I see aren't here for us at all. Perhaps they were responding to someplace else nearby.

My hands tightened around my belly, refusing to believe that I was utterly alone right now. Focusing my attention back on Hannah, I listened as she continued.

"The problem is, every time her daddy gets out of prison, he gets all nasty and violent. But you know all about that because you were here when I came into the shelter."

"I remember. You came here pretty banged up with Eva in tow. She was carrying a stuffed elephant if I recall —a purple one."

"That's right. It's her favorite color. Good memory," she said, lifting the right side of her mouth in a lopsided smile. But almost as fast as the half-grin appeared, it was gone. Frowning, she continued. "She lost that elephant a couple of months later. She was devastated—kept me up all night crying about it."

"Aww, the poor thing."

"I would have bought her a new one, but I didn't have the money," Hannah said defensively. "After you helped me out with the job here, I'd just barely managed to save enough to move out and get my own place. For a short time, everything was looking good—even if money was tight. Then the damn pandemic hit, and I don't know. Everything just got more and more expensive. I felt like I was drowning—like I couldn't do it anymore. Then, one morning, Eva was crying about wanting cereal for breakfast. I would have tried talking her into eating something different, but we didn't even have bread in the house for toast. She didn't understand that I couldn't afford it, but I still snapped at her. I came to work later that day, and all I could think about was not being able to feed my child. I just felt so helpless. Then, when I saw how Claire forgot to log out of the online banking system, I took it as a sign. I hurried up, transferred the money to my bank, then logged off. I didn't even think past that or about getting caught. All I could think about was my baby crying."

"And you just didn't want her to cry anymore."

"That's right. It was like I wasn't good enough for her. What kind of mother can't feed her kids? Eva deserves a better momma," she said. Her head dropped in defeat as she lowered the gun to her side.

I exhaled with relief when I no longer felt the hard

press of the gun, but I didn't dare move. I had to stay the course.

Just keep her talking until help arrives.

"I don't think you're a bad mom. If you were, you wouldn't care so much. You just made a mistake. I get it, Hannah. I get why you did it. You were desperate, that's all."

"The worst part is, I didn't even spend any of the money," she said bitterly. "I felt too damn guilty. I tried to figure out a way to return it, but when the neighbor told me the police had been knocking on my door with a warrant for my arrest, I knew I'd lost my chance. So, I took Eva and went to crash at a friend's house, even though it was probably only going to be a matter of time before the police found me."

"You might be right about that. They most likely would have caught up with you eventually," I said cautiously.

"When my friend found out I was in trouble for larceny, she said I couldn't stay there anymore. That made me panic because I had nowhere else to go, so I left Eva at her house and came straight here. I was hoping Claire would somehow let me give the money back and drop the charges."

My heart hurt, unable to fathom how something as simple as not having breakfast cereal had resulted in so many acts of desperation.

"I might be able to help you, Hannah. You said you didn't spend any of the money?" I asked.

She shook her head. "Not a dime."

"That could work in your favor."

"How so?"

"Well, the money and larceny charge aside, you're probably going to be in some serious trouble for holding up a building full of people tonight. However, I happen to be married to a pretty powerful guy." I paused, thinking of how Alexander would most likely react to all of this. He'd want Hannah thrown away for life just for threatening me. Resolving to having to deal with convincing him otherwise, I continued speaking. "My husband knows people—a lot of people. By default, I have many of the same connections that he does."

"Rich people tend to know everyone important," she said dryly.

"Hear me out. If you return the money, we can possibly get the charges reduced or even dropped. As for what happened here tonight, I might be able to convince the right people that it was all a misunderstanding. All I need to do is talk to the DA, Thomas Green. He and I have...." I trailed off, looking for the right words to describe my relationship with the local prosecutor who helped me in the past. "He and I have a bit of a history, and I think he'll do me this favor."

"I don't believe you."

"I'm serious. Have I ever lied to you before? The last

thing I want is for you to face jail time and have your daughter go into foster care—especially right before Christmas. I'm not saying there won't be consequences, but I can help minimize them. So, what do you say? Can the two of us walk out of here and focus on the next step?"

19

Krystina

"Y ou mean, turn myself in?" Hannah asked hesitantly.

"Well..." I trailed off as I scrambled to find the right words. I was terrified that a confirmation would have her pointing the gun at my chest once more. Nevertheless, honesty hadn't steered me wrong so far, so I stayed the course. "I'm afraid I don't see any other way. So yes, it means turning yourself in—but only so we can get this all sorted out."

I studied her face. A civil war battled in her wide, chocolate-colored eyes, torn about accepting my offer to help. When her lower lip began to tremble and tears began to fall, I held my breath. I had no idea what she was thinking, but I silently hoped the display of emotion was a sign of surrender.

Without warning, Hannah dropped to her knees. The gun fell to the ground as she brought her hands up to cover her face. When she began to sob, her cries were loud and heart-wrenching.

So many emotions swirled inside me—relief, anger, sympathy, sadness. I didn't know what to do, so I let my instincts guide me. Kneeling on the floor next to her, I discreetly kicked the gun out of reach, then draped my arm over her shoulders.

"Shhh," I whispered. "Everything will be okay."

I stroked her back while she sobbed. We stayed like that for a few moments before Hannah eventually raised her head to look at me with a tear-stained face.

"I don't know what's going to happen after I walk out of here," she said. "I know you think you can use your connections to help me, but knowing my luck, I'll still face time."

"You don't know that. I can—"

"No, listen. Please," she interrupted. "I know I fucked up, and I'll do whatever it is I have to do to make it right. If a judge wants me to volunteer my time dancing in a chicken costume in Times Square, that's what I'll do. But if he gives me prison time, I have no family to take care of my daughter. I grew up in foster care, and that can't happen to Eva. She's too good—untainted. So if I have to go away for a bit, I need to know she'll be somewhere safe. Can you make sure of that?"

I blinked, not entirely sure what she was asking of me.

"I can try, Hannah. I don't know if I'll have much sway with Child Protective Services, though."

"I doubt CPS will dare tell someone like you that you can't take Eva into your home."

My brow furrowed in confusion, and I frowned.

"Wait. Me? You want *me* to take her in?"

"Only if I have to spend time in jail. I need to keep Eva out of the system. You can understand that, can't you?"

I thought about everything Alexander had told me about his childhood. He'd spent most of his youth living in poverty. If his grandparents hadn't taken him and Justine in after the tragedy with their parents, he might have ended up lost in the system too. Given the burdens he was carrying at such a young age, who knew how he would have fared?

I momentarily considered Alexander's thoughts about possibly taking in Hannah's daughter but quickly dismissed any pondering of that. At the end of the day, I knew Alexander would want me to say whatever I had to if it meant getting out of here in one piece.

Slowly, I nodded my head. "I understand your concern. I'll do what I can, but let's just hope it doesn't come to that."

She closed her eyes, and I watched her shoulders visibly relax. It was as if she could finally breathe, knowing that her child would be cared for if anything were to happen to her. When she opened her eyes, they were clear. Her resolve was evident in her spine as if she were preparing to take on any challenge the world threw at her.

Sucking in a shaky breath, she glanced toward the door and said, "I'm ready to go out. It's time to face the music."

Not wanting to delay another second to get out of the building, I stood up from my crouched position. Hannah followed suit, and we both left the conference room.

Following the long corridor to the main vestibule, I paused just before reaching the glass doors. From my vantage point, I could see several police cars on the street in front of Stone's Hope. People in uniform lined the curb, blocking the crowd gathered behind them. I assumed the group included Claire, the staff, and the mothers and children who managed to escape earlier.

"Let me go first," I said to Hannah. "Put your hands up and follow me out."

As soon as the two of us stepped out into the cold, Hannah was promptly surrounded by police officers. Orders were shouted from my left and right, instantly sweeping me up in total chaos. Only one thing was able to bring me back into focus—a pair of piercing blue sapphire eyes.

Alex.

I'd never been so happy to see him, and my shoulders

sagged with relief. I wanted to run to him, but the rage in those gorgeous blues rooted me to the spot. His gaze was frigid and empty of the usual affection he showed me. I didn't think I'd ever seen him appear so angry. Instinctively, I reached up to replace my masks that had been hooked under my chin—not because I thought that was the sole reason for his fury, but because I thought it might give him less reason to be so mad.

Flanked by two police officers, he stood rigid with his arms behind his back. He wasn't wearing a winter coat, having only his immaculately tailored black suit jacket for warmth. His red tie was knotted with precision as usual, but there was something off about his appearance as well. He seemed uncharacteristically disheveled. I hesitantly took a couple of steps forward, only to stop again when I realized why he stood so still.

Is he in handcuffs?

My eyes widened in shock. It didn't matter if I had only done what I thought was right by coming here tonight. If he was in cuffs, there had clearly been an altercation—and it was most likely over me.

Shit.

There would be no talking Alexander from this ledge now. I may have pushed him a little too far this time. Putting one foot in front of the other, I marched toward the three men displaying a confidence that I didn't really feel. When I reached them, I looked back and forth between the two officers.

"Will someone please tell me why my husband is in handcuffs?" I demanded.

"It's because he—" one officer began.

"Never mind. The reason doesn't matter," I interrupted. "Release him, now."

The two officers looked back and forth between themselves. I was sure they were contemplating whether Alexander was worth the mountain of paperwork his arrest would bring.

Eventually, one of the officers glanced at Alexander.

"Is this your wife?" he asked him.

"It is, Officer Bailey," my husband replied through clenched teeth.

With a shake of his head, Officer Bailey moved behind Alexander. "I suppose there's no harm in letting you go. No reason for you to run into that building like a crazed lunatic anymore now, is there?"

"No, officer," Alexander said curtly. A moment later, his hands were back out in front of him. When the officers walked away, he eyed me coolly as he took turns rubbing each wrist.

"Alex, I'm so sorry," I said hurriedly. "I only came here to—"

"Stop talking," he ordered. Stepping up to me, he yanked the masks from my face, then quieted my tumbling words with a hard press of his lips. There was nothing tender about his mouth. This was an angry kiss driven by worry, fear, and relief. After a few seconds, he tore his mouth from mine and growled in a low voice, "I'm so fucking angry with you."

"I know. And I'm sorry."

"Sorry doesn't cut it. I have half a mind to take you over my knee and spank you right here—and I don't care who's around to see."

"I dare you to try it," I challenged.

"Don't provoke me, Krystina."

I angled my chin up stubbornly. "I think I have the right to provoke you all I want after the way you lied. Your need to control everything has gone way too far this time. I may have gone against you by coming here tonight, but I'm done living like a prisoner."

"What are you talking about?" he quipped.

"Don't you dare play innocent," I countered, shaking a finger at him. "You've kept me locked up in the house needlessly for months. The virus is practically nonexistent—in particularly, in the city. I've been extremely busy with holiday ad campaigns for the past three months and wasn't following the news—as you were well aware. So imagine my surprise when I popped on the news last night."

"Your point?"

"Oh, don't even consider being blasé about this! The news reported zero cases in the last seven days—zero! I know you, and I know how religiously you follow national and local news because of your businesses. Don't try to pretend you didn't know this."

"I did know. I just didn't know it would be that big of a deal to you. We agreed to take precautions to ensure your safety while we are trying to get pregnant. End of story. Not telling you about it doesn't make it a lie."

"Omission is the same as lying," I countered. As soon as the words were out of my mouth, a stab of guilt hit me. I was accusing Alexander of doing the exact thing that I was doing. I wasn't lying about my pregnancy but omitting the truth, just as he had. I was the pot calling the kettle black.

I sighed and pinched the bridge of my nose. After the stress of the past couple of hours, the last thing I wanted to do was fight with Alexander. All I really wanted was to curl up under a blanket, cocoon in the comfort of my husband's arms, and pretend as if this were all just a bad dream.

"Look, Alex. Let's just—" I stopped short when I saw Hannah being led to a police car parked about fifty feet away from where we stood. The officer who had her in his custody placed his hand on her head and guided her into the backseat. "I'll be right back."

"The hell you will," Alexander snapped, but I ignored his protests.

"Wait!" I called out to the officer. Pulling free from Alexander, I rushed over to the vehicle before the officer could close the door.

"Ma'am, I need to—"

"I just need one minute. Please, officer," I said.

"Make it quick," he warned.

Lowering my body until I was eye-to-eye with Hannah, I placed a hand on her arm.

"Hannah, I meant what I said. I will help you through this. Is there anyone I can call for you?"

"My friend, Madilyn. She has Eva. I don't know if she'll be willing to keep her overnight or longer. I don't know what's going to happen and I-I don't—" Her voice cracked, and she stopped short to choke back a sob.

"I know you're worried about your daughter. I won't let you spend the night in jail. I'll pay whatever it is to make sure you're released on bail so you can be with her."

With tear-filled eyes, she smiled and nodded.

"Thank you, Krystina. You've always been so good to me. I'm sorry for this—sorry for everything."

"Have faith. Everything will be okay. I promise."

Standing, I backed away and allowed the policeman to close the door. After he climbed into the driver's seat and drove away, I watched the car until it disappeared from sight.

Alexander stepped up next to me, his commanding presence overshadowing anything else around us.

"After all the shit you put me through, are you going to tell me what that was all about?" he asked.

The adrenaline that had pumped through my veins over the past hour had long since disappeared, and exhaustion weighed heavily on my shoulders. Yes, I was still angry with Alexander over keeping me caged, but I

also owed him an explanation—and so much more. I just
didn't have the energy to do it while standing in the snow
on a cold city street. I wanted to be home—warm and safe
in his arms. I didn't want to think about stolen money, a
virus, or risks to our baby. I wanted to just *be*, even if only
for a few minutes.

I glanced up at my husband. There was still anger in
his gaze, but there was also worry and relief etched into
his features. I loved this man with my whole heart, and if
I'd thought through this crazy idea to come to the shelter
a little better, I would have done everything so much
differently. My tendency to react first and think later had
gotten me into plenty of trouble in the past, and I knew
better.

Reaching up to cup Alexander's face, I looked at him
with pleading eyes.

"For now, let's just go home. Please. There will be
plenty of time for me to fill you in later, Alex. I promise to
tell you everything."

"Alright," he said, albeit reluctantly. Then he sternly
added, "But until you're safe at home, put that damn mask
back on your face."

I shook my head but didn't argue as I pushed the mask
back to cover my mouth and nose.

"I'm sorry that I worried you, Alex. Really, I am."

"Worried? I was scared out of my fucking mind,
Krystina. Only you would manage to land yourself in a
hostage situation. Sometimes I wonder if you're trying to

put me into an early grave," he said, sounding somewhat bewildered.

Alexander's face softened then—just a tad—but it was enough for me to know that I would eventually get a reprieve. Hiding behind the protection of the mask, I secretly smiled with relief. Alexander wasn't off the hook for the way he'd controlled and isolated me, but I knew no matter what, everything was going to be just fine.

20

Christmas Eve
Alexander

I paced back and forth in the foyer, waiting for Krystina to come downstairs. We had been all ready to go, but at the last minute, she had to hurry back up to our bedroom for something. There was nothing she could possibly need, but she'd been gone for ten minutes.

When she finally came bounding down the grand staircase, her cheeks were flushed, and there was a mischievous twinkle in her eye. My heart constricted simply from the sight of her beautiful face, and I wondered if there would ever come a day when I didn't feel like the earth was shifting beneath my feet whenever she walked into a room.

"I'm ready to go!" she announced.

"It's about time," I grumbled, but I said it with a small smile, letting her know my irritated tone was only a façade. I was just anxious to reveal the surprise I'd put together for her.

I gave Krystina a once-over to make sure she was dressed warmly enough. She had no idea about what I had in store for her. As far as she was concerned, we were just going back to the igloo near the pond to enjoy a Christmas Eve dinner that Vivian was currently preparing in the kitchen.

Reaching down, I picked up the backpack that I'd prepared earlier, then slung it over my shoulder. Krystina quirked up a brow and eyed the bag curiously.

"Santa's toy sack?" she asked.

"Something like that," I answered, tossing her a wink.

While the first few days after her little escapade into the city had been strained, we'd found our footing again. I swore that she only defied me because she knew it drove me absolutely crazy. I recalled her ire over feeling controlled just as well and I remembered how badly I wanted to take her over my knee and give her the paddling she deserved. The problem was, I was just so happy she was safe, and I found that I couldn't dole out a punishment when all I wanted to do was hold her. It was out of character for me, and I couldn't help but think it was directly related to how I'd felt when Krystina had been kidnapped a few years back. I never wanted to feel that fear again.

It didn't matter what Krystina's arguments were for going to the shelter. I didn't care if she thought it was safe or if it was an impulsive decision made out of anger at me. I still wasn't happy about the risks she took. However, my deep understanding of her generous heart allowed me to look past it—along with Hale's assurances that he would be Krystina's shadow from now on.

When we stepped outside into the cold night air, I breathed deep. The temperature had been just below freezing all week, leaving just the right amount of moisture in the air so as not to make it feel too brisk. I glanced up and saw that there wasn't a star in sight. The cloud cover and lack of wind would ensure our evening outdoors would be pleasurable.

"Do you want to walk, or do you want to take one of the golf carts?" I asked.

"Well, if our excursion ends like it did the last time, I'd prefer to skip the long walk back. Let's take a golf cart."

I smirked as I remembered how I'd barely made it to the front door without stripping her bare. It was highly unlikely that would be the case tonight, but she didn't know that.

"Good call, angel. Golf cart it is." Walking around back to the main garage, I pulled a key out of my pocket, inserted it into the exterior lockbox, then went through the security steps to open the main door.

When we entered the garage, I had to suppress a curse. Only one of the three golf carts used to navigate the property was parked along the far wall. Both ATVs were missing as well. That meant Hale must have taken them down to the pond. I glanced at Krystina, hoping she didn't notice their absence, then quickly stepped in front of her to block her view of where they would usually be parked.

Removing the backpack from my shoulders, I unzipped the top. Thankfully, Krystina was curious about what I was doing and kept her attention on me. She didn't seem to notice the missing recreational vehicles, and I internally sighed with relief.

Reaching into the backpack, I pulled out a satin scarf.

"Turn so I can tie this over your eyes," I told her.

"Alex, it's silly to blindfold me again. I already know that you have the area around the pond all decorated."

"After the surprise was ruined last time, I made some adjustments and additions. For starters, I know the lights work this time," I said with a chuckle. "Now, turn around."

Shaking her head, she did as I instructed and asked, "Did you find out why they weren't working before?"

"A critter got to the main electrical line to the shed and chewed it straight through," I explained as I tied the knot at the back of her head. Once I was satisfied it was secure, I stepped in front of her and cupped her face between my palms. Then, leaning in, I pressed a soft kiss to her lips and said, "I hope you know how much I love you."

"Mmmm…" she hummed, darting her tongue out to lick her lips as if she were searching for more of my kisses. That little action made my cock jerk to life, wanting to give her more and then some.

"Careful, angel. We'll never make it back to the pond if you don't put that tongue back in your mouth."

"Since I've forgiven you for being a neurotic control freak, does this mean you've forgiven me for leaving the house last week?" she asked with a coquettish grin.

"As furious as I was, I can't stay mad at you for long. You know that."

Taking her arm, I guided her over to the lone golf cart and helped her into the passenger side. Then, sliding into the driver's seat, I pulled a pair of noise-canceling headphones from the backpack and placed them over her ears.

"What's this?" she asked in surprise. "Am I not allowed to hear anything either?"

I chuckled, then shifted one of the ear coverings aside so she could hear me.

"Sensory deprivation, baby. You know how much I get off on that," I teased, then laughed at Krystina's quick intake of breath.

I slid the headphones back into place, then started the golf cart. Maneuvering it out into the main driveaway, I secured the garage doors once more, then began the drive back to the pond.

It had snowed this afternoon, leaving a dusting on the path. Tire tracks from the other recreational vehicles marred the pristine white and I was grateful I'd decided to put the blindfold on Krystina before we left the garage. If she saw the tracks, it might give her a clue about her surprise. Santa's sack, as she so aptly put it, still had a few more surprises in it. However, the most significant gift I had for her this Christmas wasn't something that could be wrapped or put under a tree.

When we reached the end of the path, the trees gave way to reveal the clearing around the pond, and I took my foot off the gas pedal. Looking to Krystina, I made sure her blindfold was still secure. Satisfied that she still couldn't see anything, I got off the golf cart and came around to her side to help her down.

Leading her around to the front of the cart, I placed my hands on her shoulders and held steady, my firm grip signaling that she should remain still. Turning to my head to the left, I took in the sight of Krystina's big gift.

Our closest friends, Allyson, Matteo, Bryan, and Stephen, stood huddled together next to Krystina's mother and stepfather, Elizabeth and Frank Long. Hale and my sister, Justine, were there as well. They had brought my mother to the surprise, knowing she would enjoy seeing all the Christmas lights. She sat bundled up in her wheelchair with Hale watching protectively over her, just as he always did.

I held a finger to my lips, signaling for them to be quiet. Then, reaching up, I removed the headphones from Krystina's ears.

"Give me your phone," I said to her.

"My phone?" she questioned. "Why do you need my phone?"

I huffed out an impatient breath.

"Must you question everything? Please. Just hand me your phone."

Reaching into her coat pocket, she pulled out her cell and handed it to me. After unlocking it, I searched her music library for her favorite Christmas playlist, then synced it to the Bluetooth speaker I had stashed in the backpack. I set both the speaker and phone down on the back of the golf cart just as Bruce Springsteen & The E Street Band began singing *Merry Christmas, Baby*.

Going back to Krystina, I loosened the satin knot at the back of her head. Then, before removing the blindfold completely, I leaned in and traced my lips softly over the shell of her ear.

"Merry Christmas, angel," I whispered, then let the silky material fall from her eyes.

All at once, the music was momentarily drowned by a chorus of voices.

"Merry Christmas!" everyone yelled.

Krystina blinked in confusion, almost as if she didn't

believe what she saw. She looked at the group of friends and family, then shifted her eyes to take in all the decorations dotting the clearing around the pond.

One hundred white angels circled the icy water's edge. Their brilliant lights illuminated the night. Along the path, the winter wonderland Hale and I had initially constructed had been expanded to a festival of lights that would rival some of the best in the country. I'd enlisted the help of Kimberly Melbourne, a design engineer that I frequently worked with, knowing she would be able to create everything I had envisioned. She'd brought in an entire crew to erect everything from a large-scale light-up gingerbread house to a life-sized sleigh complete with Santa and his eight reindeer. A cluster of igloos was off to the left. Red and white poinsettias lined the transparent plastic bubbles, reminding me of winter greenhouses. The plants surrounded small tables covered in red cloth, each one set for the dinner Vivian would be serving us later in the evening.

As I watched Krystina's face change from bewilderment to pure joy. The beams of light from the decorated trees fell like wishes over her face, and I knew every effort and penny spent to create this for her had been worth it.

"What...how did you..." she trailed off, seeming at a loss for words. "So many decorations and everyone is here. How... Alex, the rules. I..."

I couldn't help but laugh. It was rare to see my sassy wife struggling to speak.

"I realized that the most meaningful gifts aren't always wrapped in a bow, and I wanted to give you what you deserved. Plus, a chat with Dr. Tumblin may have swayed me to relax on the rules a bit. Of course, there are still precautions in place, but I managed to figure out a way for us to all be together."

"Alex insisted we all get tested this morning," said Elizabeth Long, sounding slightly exasperated over the inconvenience. "But we all agreed that it was a small price to pay if it meant we could have a semi-normal Christmas."

"Yes, but we still need to use common sense," I added, more as a warning to Krystina's mother. Elizabeth had been the most resistant to my rules, and I wanted to ensure she didn't forget.

"Mom, where are you staying? It's a long haul from Albany. Surely, you can't be in a hotel?"

"Alex was adamant about no hotels, so Allyson offered to put us up in your old bedroom at the apartment on Bleecker Street," Elizabeth clarified.

Krystina still seemed in shock, having done little more than shake her head in disbelief.

"I still can't believe..." she began, only to trail off again.

"I know how controlling I am, and I love that you accept that side of me," I explained. "But I recognize how much this pandemic has amplified it. I hated seeing you caged up, but I couldn't push away the worry. You've always been more social than I am, and I never once considered what so much isolation would do to you. It was slowly killing your spirit. I love you, and I just want you to enjoy your favorite time of the year. So, this is my way of compromising for the holiday."

"Just for the holiday?" she asked.

My jaw clenched, although I wasn't the least bit surprised by her challenge.

"Don't push it, angel. I can't just flip a switch on this. Baby steps, okay?"

"Alex, it's okay. I mean, we both agreed that—"

"Hold that thought until later," I interrupted. "I don't want to get into some long-winded conversation about what rules are still in place for right now. Besides, this isn't your only gift." Reaching down to the backpack sitting at my feet, I pulled out a flat package wrapped in silver and red paper and handed it to her.

"What's this?" she asked.

"This is the rest of your present, angel. Open it."

Her brow furrowed with confusion as she simply stared down at the gift.

"Krystina, the anticipation is killing me," Allyson joked. "Are you going to open it, or what?"

"Sush, Ally," Krystina scolded, but her eyes were smiling. "I still can't believe you're all here. So many people watching me is nerve-wracking!"

"I can help if you need me to," Allyson replied.

Krystina ignored her friend and focused her attention on tearing the package open. Inside was a plain manilla envelope. She eyed me with curiosity for a moment, then opened the envelope and pulled out a stack of paper.

"Twelve Dates of Christmas," she read aloud from the cover sheet.

"That's right. Today is the first date—dinner in a Christmas igloo surrounded by friends and family. Then, starting tomorrow, I have something planned for the next eleven days," I said. "First is an outing to Rockefeller Center. I got with my contacts at Tishman Speyer, and they agreed to cordon off the Christmas tree area and give us two hours of private ice time if you want to ice skate. No people around means no risks, which in turn satisfies both of us. You get out of the house and I don't have to worry. Baby steps, remember? The following day, I've arranged a private showing of the Radio City Christmas Spectacular. The Rockettes—"

"Whoa! Wait a minute here," Krystina interjected. She shook her head, seeming apprehensive.

"Angel, what's wrong?" I asked when I noticed her eyes wide with alarm.

"Nothing—everything. I mean, I can see you're trying to loosen the reins, and I appreciate that, although I'm not sure what else you have planned for the twelve dates. I mean, a private showing of the Rockettes? Aside from the fact that it's a little Vanderbilt-ish, I just think..." she trailed off, glancing around nervously as we waited for her to finish. "Don't you think it's too much?"

My eyebrows raised in surprise. That was the last thing I expected her to say.

"Krys!" Elizabeth said with exasperation. "I raised you better than that. Show some appreciation!"

Frank put his hand on his wife's arm, almost as if to remind her that Krystina was a grown woman and Elizabeth should mind her own business. Krystina, on the other hand, just pressed her lips together in a tight line. I expected her to lash out at her mother for taking such a condescending tone, but instead, a look of confusion came over my wife's face. It was surprising, as Krystina barely tolerated her mother on most days. Perhaps time and distance was exactly what she needed to find a little patience for the know-it-all, and sometimes intrusive, Mrs. Elizabeth Long.

"I do appreciate Alex's gift, mom. It's not that," Krystina said.

"Well, what is it then?" Elizabeth asked with bewilderment.

"I just..." She didn't finish her sentence as another wave of apprehension crashed over her features. Turning her attention back to me, she stared at me with worried eyes. "All of this—having everyone together and the twelve dates. Even though I don't know what the other dates entail, I can already tell how much thought you put into everything. It means so much to me—really, it does.

I'm so grateful that you carefully considered my words about feeling controlled and are making an effort. I just think I should give you my gift first, and then we can talk about whether you think your gifts are still, shall we say, safe. Okay?"

My brows pushed together in a frown. I had no idea what Krystina meant by 'safe.' I wouldn't give any of this to her without taking every possible precaution to ensure her safety.

"Alright, angel," I finally said, my curiosity overriding all else. "I guess I could use an explanation for why you seem so apprehensive. I thought you'd be happy about my gifts."

"I am but..." Looking down, she reached into her pocket and pulled out a small rectangular box wrapped in champagne-colored foil with a burgundy bow. She looked at me sheepishly, then thrust the box in my direction. "This is why I'm worried. Merry Christmas, Alex."

21

Krystina

Alexander slowly reached out, appearing almost afraid to take the present. I was sure my behavior had thrown him off, so I rushed to reassure him.

"I'm sorry. I didn't really prepare for this. It was kind of a last-minute decision. I was going to wait until Christmas morning to give this to you, but when you said we were having dinner by the pond, I wasn't sure what to expect. I didn't want to risk missing the perfect moment. It's why I went back upstairs earlier. I had to wrap this just in case I decided to give it to you early. And now, with everyone here, I can't think of a better time."

He eyed me curiously for a moment, then slid his

finger under the break in the wrapping and pulled the foil from the box. Lifting the lid, a gold triskelion key in a bed of sapphire blue satin was nestled inside. With it, there was a note card. Alexander flipped it open, and we all listened to him read it aloud.

Our family will always hold the key to my heart. Merry Christmas, Alex.

Love, Your Angel

Allyson, my mother, and Justine's simultaneous reactions were predictable.

"Awww!" cooed my best friend and sister-in-law.

"How sweet!" chimed my mother.

I held up a hand to quiet them and pointed to the box. Focusing all my attention on Alexander, I said, "Take the key out of the box and lift the satin. There's another surprise inside."

I studied his every move, memorizing every detail in his expression as he peeled back the silky layer to reveal the positive pregnancy test that sat at the bottom of the box.

His eyes widened as he registered what he was looking at. His gaze darted around to the faces of everyone present—except for me. Shifting his gaze back down to the box, a mixture of confusion and elation shown in his expression. His silence was deafening as the tension in the air grew so thick, I'd swear you could cut it with a knife. It was unnerving and I eventually couldn't take it anymore.

"Alex, say something," I finally said.

Turning, he pulled me into his arms and touched his forehead to mine. Our breaths mingled and my eyes closed as I took a moment to appreciate the silent intimacy passing between us.

Pressing a kiss to my forehead, Alexander murmured, "I almost can't believe it, and I..." His words trailed off, faltering almost as his voice cracked with emotion. "I just want to kiss you."

Tears filled my eyes and I smiled.

"So do it."

"If I do, I'm afraid I'll never stop. How long have you known?"

"I'm thirteen weeks," I whispered.

Alexander's head snapped back to look at me.

"Thirteen weeks? And you waited this long to tell me?"

"I just wanted to make sure everything would be okay because...well, you know." I didn't elaborate further since nobody except Alexander and Allyson knew about the struggles that I'd had with carrying a pregnancy to term.

"Thirteen weeks? What are you talking about, Krystina?" my mother asked, suddenly reminding me that Alexander and I weren't alone. Alexander hadn't taken the pregnancy test out of the box, so there was no way for anyone to know what our quiet conversation was about.

Turning to her and my stepfather, I grinned. "Merry Christmas! It looks like you're going to be grandparents."

"Oh my! You're pregnant!" my mother exclaimed, not bothering to hide her shock. She wasn't smiling, but rather had a look of alarm. It was almost comical. Her expression was definitely worth the price of admission.

"That's wonderful news," Frank added, knowing as well as I did that this would take a while to sink in with my mother. I was fairly certain her first thought was how she didn't think she was old enough to be called grandma.

I looked to the rest of our friends. Allyson shifted her stylish knit hat as she flipped back her golden blond hair. She was sporting a wide grin, gripping Matteo's arm with excitement. He was also smiling, but it didn't quite meet his eyes. Following the direction of his gaze, I saw he was watching Alexander with apprehension. Looking at Bryan, Stephen, Hale, and Justine, I saw similar expressions on their faces as well. Before I could inquire about why they seemed anxious, my mother spoke again.

"You're absolutely sure that you're pregnant, Krystina?" she pushed.

"Yes, mom. I'm—"

"Krystina, what about the doctor?" Alexander interrupted. "You've been quarantined to the house. With your history, you should have been going all this time and —" He stopped short, and that's when I saw the fear in his eyes. I understood it all too well. It was what had made him fall silent when he first saw the positive pregnancy test. His fear made him afraid to hope. As emotionally fragile as I'd been feeling, he'd felt every bit as unstable as I had.

"I've had regular video conference calls with my gynecologist. She even made two house calls," I assured.

"Have-have you—" he uncharacteristically faltered, his voice sounding hoarse. "Have you heard the heartbeat?"

My chest tightened, feeling as though it might burst with love for this man. I smiled softly, understanding his uncertainty. He was afraid that he'd missed out.

"No. I haven't had a sonogram yet. The doctor would like one soon, though. I was just waiting for you for that part. Besides, arranging home visits to ensure the doctor was here and gone by the time Vivian finished with her Friday errands was challenge enough. The doctor and I made it work, but there was no way I'd be able to sneak in sonogram equipment. I'm not that good," I added with a laugh.

"I wish you would have told me sooner, Krystina. I don't appreciate being left in the dark."

The hurt in his eyes was evident, causing guilt to claw at my conscious.

"I know, Alex. A part of me wanted to tell you so badly, but I wanted to be sure everything was okay first. Trust me when I say that keeping it from you was near impossible. My acting skills were definitely tested, that's for sure."

Alexander's eyebrows lifted in surprise. "When did you become so sneaky?"

"The moment I met you," I joked with a laugh. "But seriously, after all we've been through, I was only doing what I thought was best. And well, I had to be sneaky. You control everything and tend to ruin all my surprises."

"She's right about that," Matteo chimed in, and I laughed.

"Sorry, Alex. Some secrets are just meant to be kept hidden—even if only for a little while," I added.

The hard, tense lines of his shoulders relaxed, and I mentally sighed my relief. I knew he would be upset that I hadn't told him, but I could explain more about my reasoning later.

"So, Alex," Stephen said. "You don't own any guns by chance, do you?"

Alexander frowned in confusion. "Not personally. Why?"

"Because if you end up with a baby girl, I don't want to have to defend you in court. I pity any man that comes sniffing around her."

Bryan laughed and added, "If the guy who dates Alex's daughter is anything like he was with women—"

"Don't even fucking joke, man. Just don't," Alexander warned.

"What do you mean? How was Alex with women?" my stepfather asked.

Allyson snorted and I thought I heard a chuckle from Hale.

"Don't ask," Justine muttered.

I raised an eyebrow, still uncertain about how much Justine knew of Alexander's less than conventional life before me. No matter what she knew, I couldn't help but want to laugh at the idea of Frank knowing. He was a tolerant man, but somehow, I didn't think he'd be happy to learn about Alexander's kinks—or that I loved those kinks just as much. It was like I had said earlier—some secrets were just meant to be kept hidden.

Alexander was given congratulatory thumps on the back, while each guest took turns pressing their hand to my still mostly flat belly and giving me a brief hug. Each embrace felt stiff and awkward, ending just a little too quickly. I wasn't sure if everyone sensed it or just me, but it felt strange to hug people after so much time apart.

A brief wave of sadness washed over me as I thought about all the time lost, but I was able to push it away just by focusing on the smiling faces of all the people I loved. We were all together in one place for the first time in far too long. I wanted to savor the moment because I didn't know how long it would be until we were all together again.

I heard a rustling to my left and turned to see what it was. Vivian, who seemed to have appeared out of thin air, stood next to one of the golf carts arranging steaming mugs on a tray.

"Attention everyone!" she called. "I think a toast is in order. I have a nice mulled spiced wine here to warm the cockles of your heart on this chilly evening."

Everyone gathered around as Vivian doled out the warm beverage. When she got to me, I held up my hand. There was no way for her to know I couldn't drink it since she hadn't been here when it was revealed that I was pregnant.

"No thank you, Vivian. No wine for me because...well, I'm going to have a baby!" I announced, anxious to see her expression.

"Yes, I know, dear. That's why I prepared you a spiced cider instead. Here you go," she said offhandedly as she passed me a mug.

I blinked in surprise.

"But how could you know? You weren't here when I gave Alex his gift."

She looked at me knowingly.

"There's very little that gets past me. I just figured you had your reasons for staying quiet and would get around to telling me in your own time."

"Any you never said anything to Alex?" I asked incredulously.

Vivian laughed.

"I know better than to interfere with the two of you. Now, enough chatter for the moment. I have to run and finish dinner preparations. Hale," she said, turning to where Hale stood next to Alexander's mother. "The nursing staff will be down to collect Helena in just a bit. I'll have dinner ready to go in the insulated coolers to keep things hot, but I'll need your help strapping it all to the golf cart so I can deliver it all to the igloos."

"Not a problem at all, ma'am. I'll be up to the house as soon as I can," Hale replied.

I stared at the older woman, in awe over her endless energy. Perhaps Alexander was right. Maybe she didn't need an assistant after all—at least not right now.

"As Vivian said, a toast is in order," Alexander announced, raising his steaming glass mug. "After nearly two years of turmoil—socially, economically, and personally—I think I can finally move toward the light at the end of the tunnel. I may have been the last one to see it, but thankfully I have my beautiful wife to keep me in check."

"You got that right," I teased with a wink.

"We have a lot to celebrate today," Alexander continued as he moved to press his free hand to my belly. He glanced around at our guests before angling his head down to look meaningfully at me. "It's time to put the past behind us and focus on all the good ahead. To new beginnings!"

"To new beginnings!" everyone cried out in unison.

I smiled, my heart feeling full as I took a sip of my cider. It truly was a celebration of new beginnings. It seemed as if the pandemic was hopefully behind us, I was with everyone I held dear, and I had a new baby to look forward to. At that moment, I couldn't imagine life being any better.

"Why don't we take a walk around the pond and look at all the decorations?" Justine suggested.

"That's a great idea," Alexander agreed. Stepping toward me, he took my hand, and our small group began to walk.

White angels with trumpets followed the path around the pond, lighting our way through Alexander's winter wonderland. As we passed a large pine tree decorated with lights, ornaments, and bows, and topped with a large silver star, I heard Alexander's mother make a humming sound. I looked down at Helena. It wasn't unusual for her to make sounds when she was trying to find the right words to communicate, but this wasn't just random noises. It was more organized.

Her hum was quiet at first and I couldn't quite make out what it was. After a moment, she seemed to have found the rhythm and began to hum louder to the tune of *Have Yourself a Merry Little Christmas*. I glanced across the pond and realized the Judy Garland version of the song was playing from the wireless speaker that sat on the golf cart. The sound was faint at this distance, but I could hear it. Helena must have heard it as well.

Alexander stopped walking to look down at her. Hale paused too, as was customary whenever Helena reacted to anything.

Kneeling in front of his mother, Alexander took her

gloved hand in his. He had a faraway look on his face when he whispered, "I remember."

"Remember what?" I asked in confusion.

"A few weeks back, you asked me about holiday traditions," Alexander said, looking up at me. "I couldn't recall any. Did you ever end up asking Hale?"

"No. I forgot."

Hale gave us both a confused look as we waited for Alexander to elaborate.

"I remember my mother taking Justine and me to Dyker Heights to look at all the Christmas lights."

"Dyker Heights?" Frank questioned.

"It's a neighborhood in Brooklyn with the most over-the-top Christmas decorations," Alexander explained. "It's more extravagant now than it was when I was a kid, but still a sight to see. We'd take the D train to 79th Street and go house to house—and my mother would sing. Justine, do you remember doing that?"

Justine pinched her brows together as if she were trying to remember.

"I have a vague recollection of—wait!" she suddenly exclaimed. "I do remember. Her voice. It was..." Justine trailed off as tears began to fill her eyes.

"It was beautiful," Alexander finished for her.

"Like a bell," Hale added. I considered the few times I'd heard Alexander sing. I'd always thought he had a really good singing voice. Perhaps he'd inherited the talent from his mother.

"That was our holiday tradition," Alexander said, seeming lost in memory. "Every year, we would ride the subway to Dyker Heights and we'd walk house to house singing Christmas carols. I always looked forward to it. *Have Yourself a Merry Little Christmas* was her favorite and it was how we would end the night."

"It was one of the few times when we didn't have to worry about—" Justine began but stopped short.

"When we didn't have to worry about our father coming home and ruining everything," Alexander finished dryly.

"Yeah. We were just happy, you know?" Justine lifted a finger to her eye and sniffled.

"Maybe we should start the tradition again?" I suggested.

Alexander looked pointedly at me.

"Out of the question, Krystina. I am not going house to house in Brooklyn to sing in front of strangers."

"Who said anything about going to Brooklyn? There's no reason why we can't just sing right here," Allyson suggested. I smiled at my friend's ability to read my mind.

As if on cue, Helena's humming became louder. The end of the song was approaching, but I didn't want it to signal the end of our night like it had when Alexander was a child. Music had always been a form of therapy for me. I couldn't play an instrument any more than I could carry a tune—but I always said I could *feel* music, and that was exactly what I wanted to channel at that moment.

So, when the song transitioned to the next one on the playlist, I pulled my phone from my pocket to remotely turn up the volume on the speaker. Once the music was projecting more clearly across the pond, I began to sing.

"City sidewalks, busy sidewalks..."

Our friends and family didn't need any encouragement and easily picked up the lyrics to *Silver Bells*. We continued around the pond, singing as we walked. Alexander remained silent, but there was no mistaking the whisper of a smile on his face. One song transitioned into another, and it wasn't until the *Twelve Days of Christmas* by Straight No Chaser came on did Alexander finally start singing. The song was a lively a cappella that energized the entire group.

But of course, Alexander had to be different. He didn't sing any of the Christmas lyrics, but only the *Africa* mashup portion of the song.

A giggle bubbled from my lips as he pulled me to him. Circling his arms around my waist, he spun me in a circle.

"Nine ladies dancing, they were dancing for me," he sang in a ridiculously high octave that had me doubling over in laughter. *"Eight maids of milking, they were milking just for me. I had Christmas down in Africa..."*

"Thank God you're a real-estate investor, Alex," Matteo teased. "I don't think you'd make it on the big stage."

Alexander narrowed his eyes.

"That's not for you to decide, my friend." Then, to my surprise, he knelt before me and pressed his face to the flat of my stomach. Whispering in a voice that only I could hear, he said, "All that matters is that my son or daughter likes it."

Holding tight to my hips, he continued to sing, finishing out the song in a much lower tenor that suited his voice. When he returned to a standing position, he cupped my face and angled it so he could rain kisses on my cheeks, forehead and nose.

When he paused to stare directly into my eyes, a million emotions swirled in his sapphire blues—emotions that I was sure mirrored my own. My heart swelled as I waited for him to speak.

"Thank you, angel. I couldn't have asked for a better Christmas gift."

22

Christmas Day
Alexander

The sun had barely peeked over the horizon on Christmas morning, but I lay in bed wide awake. I had been for most of the night, as I couldn't seem to stop touching my wife—my pregnant wife.

Krystina was still asleep with her arm thrown over the top of her head. I slowly ran my fingers over the bend at her elbow and brushed the side of her face. Traveling down, my hand slid down to her breasts toward her stomach, taking the sheet with me and exposing her naked body. Shifting down, I lay my head on her stomach.

Although we'd been here before, it was hard to believe my wife was carrying our child.

Thirteen weeks.

This was the furthest she'd carried so far. When she told me how far along she was, I couldn't explain the terror I felt over the idea of losing another baby. Not now. Not again.

People tend to forget about the father during the whole miscarriage experience. Instead, all the focus is on the woman—as it should be. But that didn't mean a father's grief, pain, and suffering weren't real. When Krystina had lost the third pregnancy, it damn near destroyed me. I couldn't imagine either of us having to go through that ever again.

As if she sensed my apprehension, Krystina stirred awake. I glanced up to see her looking down at me. Her eyes were sleepy as she gave me a slow, lazy smile.

"Morning, handsome," she murmured.

Sliding back up her body, I pushed a stray curl from her forehead and kissed her.

"Sleep well?"

"So, so. I mean, all the excitement from the night made it difficult. I'm just happy you finally know about the baby. Keeping it a secret was killing me."

I frowned. I didn't want to be mad at her for not telling me, but she was wrong in doing so. I didn't press her about it last night only because everyone was around. It was a night for family, friends, and holiday festivities. Explanations had to wait.

I propped my head up on one elbow and looked directly into her eyes. I needed to understand.

"Why did you keep it from me, angel?"

She frowned, and her face was full of uncertainty. Yet, there was also an inexplicable amount of vulnerability that hadn't been there before—almost as if she were afraid to tell me why she held onto the secret of our baby for so long.

"We've just experienced so much loss, Alex. And well... It's hard to explain. With the third pregnancy, there was this shift in you. It went beyond just excited energy. You became involved in ways you hadn't with the first two. You were attached to the baby just as much as I was. Never in my life did I think I would hear someone like you cooing at my stomach," she said with a laugh. "It was so endearing, and although I didn't think it was possible, it made me love you even more."

"You make all of that sound like it was a bad thing."

"On the contrary, no. I loved every minute of it. It brought us impossibly closer, so much so that when we lost the baby, I was crushed by reality and just wanted to hide away for a while. But I couldn't—not when I felt *your* pain just as if it were my own. You tried to be strong, but I knew your heart was shattering into a million pieces. I did these frantic web searches, trying to figure out who, when, how, and why me. I felt like I'd let you down, as if—" She stopped short, her voice cracking. "It felt as if I'd failed you."

My jaw tightened. It angered me to know that she had been carrying around all that guilt.

"It wasn't your fault, Krystina. You know that. I was the one who didn't protect you. It was—"

"No, Alex," she said, placing her finger over my lips to silence me. "It wasn't your fault. It wasn't the fault of either of us. These things just happen."

I took hold of her finger and kissed the tip, hoping with every fiber of my being that it never happened again.

"I think a part of me knew you were pregnant," I confessed.

She blinked in confusion. "What do you mean?"

"There had been little signs, and I know your body. I noticed the slight changes to your breasts and other areas, but I was just afraid to voice it aloud. I can't explain it. I felt like if I said anything, it would be tempting the Fates. Those fickle bitches hate me, so I thought it was better not to dare even hope."

I stared into the endless depths of her deep, chocolate brown eyes. They shone with tears and unmistakable love. She reached up to brush my sleep-tasseled hair to the side. I caught her wrist and kissed the center of her palm. We shared a moment of gratitude and hope, neither one of us having to say a word. We didn't have to because we just knew what the other was thinking. Hope was fragile, and we were both clinging precariously tight to it.

"No more lies, angel—even if it's just omitting the truth. Promise?"

"I'll promise if you do," she replied.

"I promise. When I found out you had left me in the dark, I...." I trailed off as I tried to explain all that I was feeling. I had so many questions, yet I didn't know where to begin. So, I decided to start with something basic first. "How have you been feeling over the past three months?"

"Honestly, not too bad at all. I had morning sickness, as expected, but it's pretty much gone now. I'm more emotional. I seem to cry at everything, and I hate crying. It's exhausting. Oh, and I'm really horny, too. So there's that," she added with a slight eye roll.

The corners of my mouth twitched.

"Is that so?"

"Yes. Ridiculously horny. I don't know why, but I just seem to want sex all the time with this pregnancy," Krystina admitted as she traveled a fingernail over my pectorals and down the length of my abdomen. I hissed in a breath when she reached the V between my hips and then trailed her finger back up.

"Is that why you've been pushing the playroom so much?" I asked.

"It could be," she coquettishly replied.

I shook my head and sighed, thinking of how many times I was so fucking hard for her that all I wanted was to take her in the playroom and release my dominance. I wanted to own her—to order her to her knees and feel her nails digging into my thighs as she took me in her mouth. I wanted her cries, her pleading, her pain, and her pleasure. When she gave me her submission in the playroom, I became the beast to her beauty, and it was something I treasured. Giving it up—even if it was temporary—hadn't been easy, but it was necessary.

"Looking back, I'm glad I never gave in to you, angel. You understand the risks, right?"

She nodded. "I do, and I agree. We've been through too much, and we don't need to take any unnecessary chances. There will be plenty of opportunities to use the playroom after the baby is born."

"After the baby is born...."

This was real. It was really happening.

I felt my insides tighten, feeling equally awestricken and terrified at the same time—awestricken over the miracle we'd been given and terrified that I wouldn't be able to adequately protect my wife and child.

No matter what I did, there would always be risks. It reminded me of Krystina's biological father lurking in the city. While it very well could mean nothing, it was just another example of the many things I had to worry about. Then there was the paparazzi. There was sure to be a full-out tabloid frenzy once they found out Krystina was pregnant, and it scared me to know I might not be willing to protect our child from it. All I knew was that I would kill before allowing anyone to harm my wife or child.

Sitting up straight, I lowered a hand to Krystina's

stomach and looked meaningfully down at her. She was the most beautiful woman I'd ever laid eyes on. Sometimes I wondered if the Fates had thrown so much shit at me for a reason. Perhaps if I hadn't gone through it all, I wouldn't appreciate Krystina as much as I did.

My throat clogged with emotion, and I almost couldn't speak. Her devotion to the family we were about to create was overwhelming, and not a moment went by when I wasn't grateful that she'd chosen to give herself to me.

I took a deep breath, cupped her face with my other hand, and allowed the words from my heart to flow freely.

"I thanked you last night, but I want to say it again. Thank you for this gift, angel. You truly are my past and my present, and now you've given me our future."

To be continued...

I hope you enjoyed the lighter side of Krystina & Alexander in *Wishing Stone*! This Christmas novel was meant to be the calm before the storm. The darkest part of their story is yet to come! Will they finally get what their hearts desire, or will the Fates give them a challenge that will break them?
Find out in *Breaking Stone*, the steamy and heart-wrenching conclusion to *The Stone Series*.

SUBSCRIBE TO DAKOTA'S NEWSLETTER

My newsletter goes out twice a month (sometimes less). It's packed with new content, sales on signed paperbacks and Angel Book Boxes from my online store, and giveaways. Don't miss out! I value your email address and promise to NEVER spam you.

SUBSCRIBE HERE: https://dakotawillink.com/subscribe

BOOKS & BOXED WINE CONFESSIONS

Want fun stuff and sneak peek excerpts from Dakota? Join Books & Boxed Wine Confessions and get the inside scoop! Fans in this interactive reader Facebook group are the first to know the latest news!

JOIN HERE: https://www.facebook.com/groups/
1635080436793794

MUSIC PLAYLIST

Thank you to the musical talents who influenced and inspired *Wishing Stone*. Their creativity and holiday magic helped me bring Krystina and Alexander to life.

Baby, It's Cold Outside by Dean Martin
It's Beginning to Look a Lot Like Christmas by Michael Bublé
Song for a Winter's Night by Sarah McLachlan
Winter Sound by Of Monsters and Men
That's Christmas To Me by Pentatonix
Ave Maria by Tadeusz Machalski
Run Rudolph Run by Chuck Berry
Merry Christmas Baby by Bruce Springsteen & The E Street Band
Have Yourself a Merry Little Christmas by Judy Garland
Silver Bells by Tony Bennett
Twelve Days of Christmas by Straight No Chaser

To listen to Krystina's complete Christmas Playlist of more than 60 songs, check out the *Wishing Stone* song list on Spotify!

ABOUT THE AUTHOR

 Dakota Willink is an award-winning *USA Today* Bestselling Author from New York. She loves writing about damaged heroes who fall in love with sassy and independent females. Her books are character-driven, emotional, and sexy, yet written with a flare that keeps them real. With a wide range of publications, Dakota's imagination is constantly spinning new ideas.

Dakota often says she survived her first publishing with coffee and wine. She's an unabashed *Star Wars* fanatic and still dreams of getting her letter from Hogwarts one day. Her daily routines usually include rocking Lululemon yoga pants, putting on lipstick, and obsessing over Excel spreadsheets. Two spoiled Cavaliers are her furry writing companions who bring her regular smiles. She enjoys traveling with her husband and debating social and economic issues with her politically savvy Generation Z son and daughter.

Dakota's favorite book genres include contemporary or dark romance, political & psychological thrillers, and autobiographies.

AWARDS, ACCOLADES, AND OTHER PROJECTS

The Stone Series is Dakota's first published book series. It has been recognized for various awards and bestseller lists, including *USA Today* and the *Readers' Favorite* 2017 Gold Medal in Romance, and has since been translated into multiple languages internationally.

The *Fade Into You* series (formally known as the *Cadence* duet) was a finalist in the *HEAR Now Festival Independent Audiobook Awards*.

In addition, Dakota has written under the alternate pen name, Marie Christy. Under this name, she has written and published a children's book for charity titled, *And I Smile*.

Also writing as Marie Christy, she was a contributor to the Blunder Woman Productions project, *Nevertheless We Persisted: Me Too*, a 2019 *Audie Award Finalist* and *Earphones Awards Winner*. This project inspired Dakota to write *The Sound of Silence*, a dark romantic suspense novel that tackles the realities of domestic abuse.

Dakota Willink is the founder of Dragonfly Ink Publishing, whose mission is to promote a common passion for reading by partnering with like-minded authors and industry professionals. Through this company, Dakota created the *Love & Lace Inkorporated* Magazine and the *Leave Me Breathless World*, hosted ALLURE Audiobook Con, and sponsored various charity anthologies.